AMISH COUNTRY UNDERCOVER

KATY LEE

LOVE INSPIRED SUSPENSE
INSPIRATIONAL ROMANCE

LOVE INSPIRED® SUSPENSE
INSPIRATIONAL ROMANCE

ISBN-13: 978-1-335-40261-5

Amish Country Undercover

This edition published by arrangement with Harlequin Books S.A.

For questions and comments about the quality of this book, please contact us at CustomerService@Harlequin.com.

Love Inspired
22 Adelaide St. West, 40th Floor
Toronto, Ontario M5H 4E3, Canada
www.Harlequin.com

Printed in U.S.A.

Grace had a gentle way with the horses that Jack found sweet.

But not enough to walk away.

"I'll round the other horse up," he said. "Before he's long gone."

"Please do find him." Grace worried her lower lip. "I don't want another animal in these people's hands. I won't let it happen. And I need to get the others back from them."

"How do you plan to do that? Do you know who his boss is?"

"No, but I'll be ready when he comes back." She took slow steps out of the woods and hobbled on her own toward her house.

Jack moved in a hurry to take her arm again. "You don't get it. He has to kill you or be killed. His boss will require it. You're not safe until I know who he's working for."

"How will you find out?"

"I don't know yet, but at least I know one thing beyond a reasonable doubt."

"What's that?

"Innocent or not, the danger has only begun for you. And it's nothing you can be ready for."

Katy Lee writes suspenseful romances that thrill and inspire. She believes every story should stir and satisfy the reader—from the edge of their seat. A native New Englander, Katy loves to knit warm, wooly things. She enjoys traveling the side roads and exploring the locals' hideaways. A homeschooling mom of three competitive swimmers, Katy often writes from the stands while cheering them on. Visit Katy at katyleebooks.com.

Books by Katy Lee

Love Inspired Suspense

Warning Signs
Grave Danger
Sunken Treasure
Permanent Vacancy
Amish Country Undercover

Roads to Danger

Silent Night Pursuit
Blindsided
High Speed Holiday

Wherefore seeing we also are compassed about with so great a cloud of witnesses, let us lay aside every weight, and the sin which doth so easily beset us, and let us run with patience the race that is set before us.

—*Hebrews* 12:1

To the families who love those who can no longer remember.

ONE

The hay crunched beneath a heavy foot, snapping Grace Miller to high alert. Earlier that night, she had thrown the straw across her barn floor as an alert system to tell her when the thief arrived. Now her makeshift alarm had sounded. She tensed, ready to catch him in the act this time.

Twice now, Grace had lost her father's newly purchased horses. The thought of having to explain a third to the church elders and lose her *daed*'s job gave her the strength she needed to confront the thief now—even if no Amish woman would ever think of doing such a hazardous and *ferhoodled* thing.

From her hiding place in the far back stall, Grace quietly shifted from her sitting position onto her bare feet. She gripped her long blue skirt and matching apron in her fists and readied herself to spring up into action. She had a horse thief to catch.

Or most likely Leroy Mast.

Leroy had been pestering her to continue their courting, which had been put on hold six months ago when her mother passed away. But now Grace's *daed*'s illness had propelled her into his role as the horse trader in the Amish community of Rogues Ridge, Kentucky. And if the bishop found out how far along Benjamin Miller's Alzheimer's had progressed, she would also be forced into another role in her community—most likely as a *maidal* woman in need of a husband. Just what Leroy wanted.

But did *she*?

Not if Leroy thought stealing her father's horses would endear her to him. That wouldn't be the type of *mann* she wanted—*if* she wanted one at all.

The hay crackled again as the intruder moved toward the horses in their stalls—here to take her life as she knew it away from her. If the intruder was Leroy Mast, he would find out right now that she was certain sure not having any of it—or him.

Listening carefully, waiting for the most opportune time to make her presence known, Grace leaned forward, hoping to tell when the thief reached the first horse's stall. She turned an ear to detect any sound but heard only silence.

Holding her breath to be as quiet as possible led to aching lungs, and she had to refill them, realizing the only thing she could hear was her heart pounding in her ears. No other sounds drifted her way, not even the flapping lips of the sleeping horses. She felt *ferhoodled* at her slip. She must have simply imagined the crunching. Maybe it had been one of her horses shifting in its sleep.

That had to be it, she figured.

With a disgruntled sigh, Grace eased back onto her makeshift bedding. The pitchfork she'd used to fluff the hay earlier now leaned against the back of the wooden stall. Her white organdy *kapp* lay on the lumpy sack she had propped up to use as a pillow. Catching a thief in the act was proving to be a long and tiring endeavor, and most likely a ridiculous waste of time for an amateur like herself. There was a reason the English called on their police for this type of work. But not the Amish. They shied away from involving law enforcement in their business. Even if Sheriff Maddox had repeatedly made his willingness to help her known, she would not take him up on his offer. Ever since her *mamm* died in the buggy accident, the sheriff learned about her *daed*'s illness and took it upon himself to check in. He came by after the first theft occurred and wanted her to report it. But she could handle this on her own, even if it took all night.

Scooping up her *kapp,* she settled it back on her head and tied it in place. There would be no more dozing. She had to keep her wits about her if she hoped to succeed without involving the local law enforcement or the elders. Calling on either of them would bring her *daed*'s illness to Bishop Bontrager's attention. Grace held out hope her father's illness wouldn't grow worse.

Thinking about Benjamin Miller had Grace frowning and biting her lower lip to halt any more tears. Nighttime was the hardest. She didn't think it could be so, but most nights she spent thinking about and planning for what all his needs would require of her the next day.

But there never seemed to be adequate planning for what the day would bring.

By the time the sun shone over the ridge that shadowed her farmhouse and cornfields, Grace would find herself exhausted, with no rest in sight.

"Please, *Gött*, help me keep him safe," she whispered. "Help me to know what to do and how to protect and care for him." *And help him not to forget me anymore.*

The crunch came again.

Grace's nerves shot back to full alert. She was certain sure that she wasn't alone, after all. And in all the time she had relaxed, the thief had been creeping closer. There was no time to prepare. Grace quickly reached for the pitchfork with both hands, and in one movement, jumped to her feet and came running out of her stall.

"Leroy Mast, you leave my horses alone!" she yelled. Her voice carried weight and authority.

Except it was not Leroy who stood before her. It wasn't an Amish man at all. Because no Amish man would ever hold a gun in his hand, never mind point it at someone.

Grace had expected to see Leroy, or perhaps a young Amish boy pranking her. Perhaps an elder setting her up for her own good, so the bishop could give her father's job as the horse trader to an Amish man, a much more suitable choice than her.

But none of her ideas matched the grave reality before her.

All she could focus on was the black barrel of the handgun less than two feet from her eyes. Its ominous closeness meant nothing compared to the speed of the bullet that could come through it and sink into her flesh. Being Amish, she'd never fired a gun, but sometimes hunting was necessary, and her *daed* had a shotgun for such a case.

Oh, why didn't I think to grab that, instead of this pitchfork?

Because I never dreamed this would happen.

"That's where you're wrong," the man aiming the gun on her said in a sad tone. "These are not your horses."

Cautiously, Grace glanced up into the face of the gunman. In the dim light of moonbeams filtering through the windows and door, she could make out black, shaggy hair beneath a cap, but his eyes were in shadow behind the gun. Without seeing his face, she couldn't tell why his tone of voice didn't match his threatening stance.

A quick glance down showed he was dressed in full black attire, from his booted feet to the cap. Dark and sinister, maybe, but his deep voice didn't correspond to the dark clothing, either. He sounded disappointed in her.

"I really wished I was wrong about you," he said. He even sighed and shook his head.

More cues that didn't match up.

Grace couldn't follow his words. In the moment, her brain struggled to compute the whole scene, never mind what he meant about being wrong about her. The only thoughts running through her mind were of escape.

In her peripheral vision, she saw the heads of the horses, watching from their stalls. She silently prayed for their protection as her gaze swung back to the gun. Grace became aware of a large lump growing in her throat. She tried to swallow, but her mouth was dry. She finally managed to gasp, "The sheriff knows."

The words were meant to warn the man and cause him to run, but instead, he gave a short laugh. His head lifted a bit as the jovial sound slipped from his lips.

That's when she saw he wasn't alone.

The silhouette of another gunman at the door also had his gun aimed right at her. She couldn't make out his face at all, but she could tell by his outline that he wore a cowboy hat perched low on his head, and he was much shorter than the man in front of her. But height didn't matter when one had a gun.

"What do you want?" Grace whispered, as her gaze flitted between the two men. Fear threaded through her words even as her hands tightened around the handle of the pitchfork. "Are you the ones stealing the horses?"

"Ones?" the man in front of her said and turned his head to look behind him.

In that instant, Grace had a choice to make. Stand and be shot or make a run for it. With the pitchfork still in her grasp, she took the opportunity to thrust it at the man in front of her. As he stumbled back, she veered around him, heading for the side door.

Two gunshots rang out behind her. Grace ducked her head as the bullets whooshed by her and splintered the wood frame of the door she ran toward. Two shots meant for her that missed their mark, but there would surely be more that might not. She could not stop running.

She reached the door and flung it wide, bursting out into the pitch darkness just as multiple gunshots went off. Throwing herself to the ground with her hands up over her head, she felt the hard gravel bite into her cheek. But adrenaline had her moving again, scuttling forward a few feet with her head low. Then she lifted her face with the goal of seeking safety. The refuge of her home was straight ahead…but still so far. The structure was dark, with no candles or lanterns burning in the windows. Grace prayed for it to stay that way.

But nothing was going the way she had planned tonight, for the upstairs bedroom in the far right corner lit up as a lantern's flame burned bright.

The gunshots had awoken her father.

More shots rang out behind her, and Grace began to run even before she stood up completely. She had to get to him before these men did. Nothing could stop her, not even the blasts behind her.

With her head bent low, she scrunched up her long dress and apron in her hands and ran all the way to the porch stairs. Tiny rocks flew up with each step and hit the backs of her calves. The hard wooden boards of the stairs scraped her bare feet when she reached them and took them two at a time. The door beckoned; she was almost there. But just as she reached the door, it swung wide and Benjamin Miller blocked her way.

Grace barreled into her father's chest with a loud *oof.* "*Daed*! Get down!" she gasped. She tried to push him back.

"Intruder!" her father hollered. Anger filled his face as he stared at her.

Tears of fear filled Grace's eyes. "Please, *Daed.* Get back inside." She pushed on his chest with all her might, but even in his weakened condition she couldn't budge him.

He leaned close and yelled in her face, "Intruder! Get off my land!"

Grace wanted to cry at his lapse of memory of her, but then another gunshot went off behind her. Desperate, she grabbed her *daed*'s bearded face and forced him to look into her eyes. "*Daedi*, it's me, *ya*? It's your Grace. Your daughter." She willed him to see her, rising up on her tiptoes to get closer.

"Was ist letz?" Benjamin Miller squinted at her in a fogged state. "Grace?"

"*Ya*, it's Grace. *Komm*. We have to get inside." She pushed him again, and this time he allowed her to steer him backward into the safety of their home. Grace slammed the door behind them just as another shot rang out in what had become a nightmare of a night.

But this wasn't a dream Grace could wake up from. Just like her father's illness, it was a trial she would have to face head-on—and alone.

Jack Kaufman held his gun close and ready to fire again. A simple arrest for a horse theft had turned dangerous. As an FBI special agent, he was put on this case when an anonymous caller from the local racetrack reported a stolen horse. A little digging and Jack found the missing thoroughbred at an overseas illegal betting operation. The transporting of the animal across borders brought the theft into his jurisdiction, so here he was in a sleepy little Kentucky town planning to close this case tonight. He had hoped to make his arrest and get back to fighting some tougher crimes.

Boy, did I misjudge that.

Never had he thought he would walk straight into a

shootout on an Amish farm. He also never thought a pretty Amish woman would be involved. Any Amish, for that matter.

"Never a dull moment on this job," he mumbled, and scanned the tree line for the gunman who had nearly taken him out, back in the barn. He grimaced at how close he had come to lights out. A glance in the direction of the farmhouse had Jack wondering if the woman had fared as well. He shouldn't care, since it was her partner who could have killed him. Whether she was hurt or not, he would deal with her after he apprehended the shooter.

He shifted position to behind the outhouse, closer to the forest. No shot went off, and he wondered if the guy was long gone. Jack silently scoffed at the idea of the woman teaming up with this bad guy with a gun. No Amish person he'd ever known dealt with guns. He hoped he lived to find out her reason, and it better be good.

For now, he had to figure out if the shooter was still out there gunning for him.

Jack crouched low and patted the ground with his free hand, still holding his gun at the ready. His fingers brushed against hard dirt. He stretched farther until he felt a rock. Throwing it might expose his body to the shooter more than he wanted, but it would be worth the risk if an ensuing gunshot determined the guy's position.

He located two good-sized stones, and after tucking one in his jeans pocket, he searched for a safe place to throw the other, one where a bullet wouldn't hit anyone.

A shadowed clearing near more trees and the towering cliff seemed to be the best.

In as silent a motion as he could manage, Jack hurled the rock toward the clearing and quickly stepped back into the protection of the small structure. He listened for the smack and roll of the rock against the hard earth. Then he braced for the reaction.

Nothing.

Seconds ticked into minutes before he tried again, with the second stone.

When only the silence of the night followed, he figured his shooter had hightailed it out of here.

For now.

The man would be back for the horse that the woman had stolen for him that day at the racetrack. Earlier, at the Autumn Woods Ranch and Racetrack, Jack had watched her tie the horse to her buggy and drive away without anyone realizing she had just stolen a thoroughbred right out from under their noses.

No one suspected the thief to be a pretty, demure Amish woman. But her little conniving and criminal operation would end tonight—before someone *did* get killed.

This woman had no idea who she was in cahoots with. They would surely kill her when they had no more use for her. She had to be *ferhoodled* if she thought otherwise.

Jack snickered at his use of a word he hadn't uttered for nearly eight years. Not since his Amish days before—

He pushed the thought away and made his way back

to the barn. His path was now clear to get the horse he was here to collect.

Right inside the door, he located a lantern, and soon had it lit and burning. Some things were like riding a bicycle, even the bicycles he hadn't been allowed to ride back where he had lived. Most Amish communities felt the commercially produced bicycles were too worldly and too fast, and opted instead for simple, two-wheeled scooters they could stand on.

Either way, those days were long gone and would never return, if he had something to say about it.

Jack held the lantern high to peruse the individual stalls. He counted three horses. One had to be the horse the woman had stolen earlier from the track. Were the others also stolen thoroughbreds? Just how deep was she into this heist? How many more had she taken and sold before someone realized?

The dim light showed each animal was a beautiful creature. The trader knew how to pick a good horse.

Or steal one.

"Hey there," Jack said in a soothing tone, so as not to spook the creature he approached first. He lifted his free hand to caress the side of the horse's head and was greeted with a soft snicker. "That's it. Just let me see your lip."

Jack lifted the equine's upper lip to reveal the permanent identification number tattooed above the row of teeth.

Not one of the numbers he was looking for. Not even the right kind of horse.

This was a standardbred, not one of the stolen thoroughbreds.

Jack took his lantern to the next stall and repeated the routine. This horse also allowed him access without a snub.

And proved to not be the stolen property.

A niggling doubt crept into his mind. Had he been wrong about the woman? Maybe he had missed the real thief because she had caught his eye for some reason.

Jack chided himself for thinking such a thing. An Amish woman was not for him. No woman was while he was on the case.

But he had to admit to himself that Grace Miller was a beautiful woman. Her hair matched the stunning chestnut color of the horse before him, but it was her wide blue eyes that drew attention to her pretty face. Why she wasn't already married was beyond him. Most Amish couples settled down at a young age. She had to be nearing twenty-five. *So what happened?*

"None of my concern," he muttered, answering his own wandering thoughts. He focused on the task at hand. Finding the thief.

Jack moved to the last horse in the barn and stopped short.

"I think we have a winner," he whispered, and paused to observe the stoic horseflesh before him. Even before Jack held out a hand to touch the smooth, sleek neck of the animal, he knew he was looking at a thoroughbred. This one demanded respect just with the tilt of his head. His coat rippled with tension. "I know it was loud in here tonight," Jack said, speaking with reverence. "But you'll be home in your own stall soon. I promise."

Jack eased his hand slowly toward the muzzle and

was glad when the horse deemed him worthy to touch him further. A quick lift of the lip revealed the correct numbers and letter configuration he'd been looking for.

Jack let the horse go and stepped back. A growing disappointment percolated through him. A glance in the direction of the house was followed by a frown. "And someone else will be getting a stall tonight. But hers will be at the county's holding cell."

Jack put the lantern up on the ledge of the stall and grabbed some tack. He opened the door and slowly approached the equine with palms up. The horse stepped back, but only once. Jack secured the lead quickly and had him out of the stall and the barn within moments.

Jack's waiting truck and trailer were hidden at the end of the drive, as he hadn't wanted to reveal his presence until he knew if the stolen horse was really here. He needed to call his supervisor and relay the events, but until any other missing horses were found, Jack wanted to wait. His best course of action would be to bring the woman in and get her to talk about their whereabouts.

Jack brought the horse to the trailer and loaded him up. He moved his truck to the house and prepared to make his arrest. Sitting behind the wheel here in the farmyard reminded him how different his current life was from his past.

But once he entered the farmhouse, how much of his past would come back? He wanted none of it.

After locking the truck up, he made his way up the steps and knocked hard on the door. "Open up! FBI! I have a warrant for your arrest. Don't make me come in there." *Please, don't make me come in there.*

TWO

"Arrest?" The appalling word felt foreign to Grace's lips as she repeated what the gunman had just announced.

Gunman or lawman?

She peered out from the side of the curtain to see the looming shape of the man she'd faced in the barn now on her porch. Her mind couldn't comprehend what all these horrific events were about, and she had no plans to open the door to ask this gunman or lawman or whoever he was to explain.

"Go away!" she yelled. "You should know the sheriff knows all about you." It wasn't a total lie. Sheriff Maddox knew about one of the thefts, so he would know there would be a thief, as well.

Just maybe not one so menacing.

"And the FBI knows all about you." The gunman's response was quick and nonchalant. "The sheriff won't be able to stop me from taking you and your *daed* away."

Daed?

With a gasp of horror, Grace pressed her back

against the wall and glanced over at her father, in his chair at the table. He looked so small now, hunched over with fear and confusion on his face.

"I won't let them take you," she said to him. "I promise."

"I know you don't like to consort with the law—" the voice came from behind the door again "—but it's best if you open the door. Resisting arrest won't go well for you in court."

"How do I know you're telling the truth? How do I know you're really the police?" she asked. In the next second she heard a tap on the window beside her.

Grace slipped aside the curtain just enough to see a badge and a small flashlight on a phone illuminating it. *Federal Bureau of Investigation... Special Agent Jack Kaufman.*

The light beam moved to the tall man's face.

They were a match.

Her breath picked up its pace at her dilemma, and she said the first thing that came to her mind. "Please don't take my *daed.*" It felt like begging, but that was the only choice she appeared to have left. "You can take the horses, but please leave us alone."

"That's not how this works. I watched you steal that horse today from Autumn Woods. There's nothing you can say to make me not take you in. You're all under arrest. And that includes your partner with the gun back there, when I catch him. And believe me, I'll catch him."

"My partner?" Now Grace was even more confused. But another feeling rose to the surface in a rush before she could temper it. The audacity of this man to accuse her of consorting with someone with such evil intentions as murder! Grace grabbed the doorknob. "He was with you, not me. How dare you?"

"Grace, a soft answer turns away wrath," Benjamin called from the table in a shocked and concerned voice. He stood up abruptly, knocking over his ladderback chair with a crash. The sound of that and her father's rightful reminder brought Grace back to her senses. Opening the door to set this man straight would only put them in more danger.

"Thank you, *Daed,* for reminding me. I'll be certain sure to keep my mind at peace, even in the midst of such danger."

"*Ya*, we must always strive for that peace of mind, Gracie."

A burst of hope caused Grace to smile at her *daed.* His moment of clarity was a glimpse into the man that she knew was still inside him. His response was lucid and insightful when he cautioned her to keep her calm. These moments made her forget about all the times he didn't recognize her.

Until the next time.

Was he even aware of them? Or would it be only Grace who would bear the burden of watching Benjamin Miller become lost in his own mind?

"Open the door, miss." The lawman spoke again, and it didn't sound like he was asking.

Grace stared at the doorknob she still held in her hand. Indecision paralyzed her. Never had she had to decide between two perils.

A blast sounding in the distance jolted her, but immediately afterward the window she stood beside shattered inward, knocking her to the floor.

Grace let out a scream as her body hit the wood planking. She rolled over onto her belly and started crawling toward her father. "Get down, *Daed*!"

The doorknob rattled. "Grace!" the man outside yelled. "Are you hurt?"

Grace hadn't even thought to examine herself. She only wanted to get to her *daed*. "N-no, I don't th-think so," she said, glancing down in panic.

"Please, open the door." The demand in his voice had been replaced with concern…and maybe some fear, she thought. He could have been killed if the bullet had hit him.

And still could be.

Grace pushed herself up on her knees and scrambled to the door, her long skirt protecting her from the scattered shards of glass. As soon as she unlocked it the man pushed it wide, and Grace fell onto her back, peering up at his towering figure. Her gaze lit on his drawn gun, once again leveled at her.

"Stay down!" he commanded and slammed the door behind him. His booming authority sent a spike of fear through Grace. Had she made the right choice, letting him in? Or were she and *Daed* in even more danger now?

The moonlight filtered through the windows, casting shadows on the large interior of the Amish home. The door from the porch opened into the *sitzschtopp*, the living room, and from there the kitchen opened off to the side, much like the homes he remembered. The Amish woman and her father sat together against that wall.

At the racetrack, he had determined her to be in her midtwenties, with light brown hair pulled back tight beneath her white *kapp.* With no one else in the house, it seemed he was right about her being unmarried, especially if her community followed the same rules as his, with the white *halsduch* cape worn over her dress. But that was a long time ago. Perhaps things had changed in eight years.

The Amish, change? No, not possible. He scoffed at the idea and got back to work.

"Stay where I can see you," he instructed, keeping to the side of the broken window. He scanned the tree line, his gun at the ready. The shooter had circled back. Jack should have expected he would return for what he'd come for. The guy couldn't go back to his boss without the horse. "I can't believe I can't turn my back on an Amish woman. Never would have believed it. I've been assigned to investigate your horse theft operation."

Jack looked at Grace Miller and shook his head in disappointment. "What were you thinking when you decided to join the operation with these thieves?"

Grace rubbed her father's hand to keep him calm, but her chin lifted in defiance. "I don't know what you mean by 'join the operation.' I didn't join anything."

"Partner. Alliance. *Bintness.*" Jack said the last word in her Pennsylvania Dutch language and saw her face contort in shock over him knowing it. He looked away from her inquisitive stare and glanced at the elderly Amish man beside her.

Benjamin Miller rubbed his straggly gray beard,

which bobbed as he opened and closed his mouth in confusion. Did the man not know his daughter was a horse thief? "Mr. Miller, I'm sorry to tell you this, but your daughter has been caught stealing a horse. With my own eyes I saw her take the animal out of the stable." He looked back at Grace and said, "But if she cooperates and tells me who she is stealing for, I might be able to get my supervisor to cut her a deal. Right now, I want the guy who nearly clipped me back there in the barn, and again on the porch. Thankfully, he's a bad shot, or my blood would be all over your property now."

The Amish woman's eyes glittered so fiercely Jack thought he was about to experience an Amish person resisting arrest. Never would he have believed it, growing up. Didn't they abhor fighting in all cases?

But could this Amish woman be different? After all, she had attacked him in the barn with the pitchfork.

"I have no idea what you're talking about," Grace said. "That man was *your* partner, not mine. In case you didn't notice, you both had your guns pointed at *me*. The only people working together here are the two of you."

Jack had to admit that something didn't add up. But that didn't mean he was about to turn around and let this woman continue running a horse theft ring. "Except I saw you take the horse, and the thoroughbred is right outside, on your property."

Grace pointed to the barn. "*My* horses are not stolen. I purchased them all fair and square. But someone has been coming here at night and stealing them from *me*. And when I say someone, I mean *you* and *your* partner."

"That man was not my partner. I don't have a partner. I work solo. Do you? Or do you have a team?" Jack crossed his arms and spread his legs wide, awaiting her response.

Grace pursed her lips. "I don't know how else to tell you this, but you have the wrong person. I am not stealing from Autumn Woods. I would never do that. They have been good to my father for years and his *daed* before him. And now to me, since I took over the dealings."

Jack glanced at Mr. Miller again. The man mumbled something incoherent. He was obviously unable to handle the role of an Amish horse dealer, but Jack struggled with the idea that the elders would allow Grace to take over.

Something was amiss.

"How long have you been working in your father's place?" he asked.

Grace's bravado dispersed in an instant. Obvious pain washed over her shadowed face as she glanced her father's way, but when she turned back to Jack, he saw worry had replaced the pain—more worry than when he had told her he was here to arrest her.

Something really was amiss.

Grace shook her head. "I'm not answering any of your questions. My *daed*'s business isn't your concern."

"It is if you're stealing horses."

"I have the papers to these animals."

"You may have papers, but they don't all match. At least one of those horses was stolen, and I've already loaded him into my trailer."

In the next instant, Grace let go of her father's hand and jumped to her feet. "I'm telling you the tru—"

Another gun blast cut her off, and Jack dived toward her. Before he reached her to cover her, yet another shot went off. They were coming from outside, but didn't appear to be aimed their way. Still, he tried to pull her down. But Grace Miller held firm.

Then her face reflected what she was looking at: a golden glow coming from the yard.

Jack turned to the window, to see flames burst from the barn door.

"The horses!" Grace yelled, and passed him in a flash.

"It's not safe," Jack said, and stretched out his arm to attempt to hold her back. But there was nothing he could do to stop the woman from racing into danger.

"Get off my property!" Mr. Miller hollered in confusion from behind, as Grace ran out the door and onto the porch. "All of you!"

Benjamin Miller was obviously suffering from some illness like dementia. Grace would need a lot of money to give him the care he needed, especially with no health insurance, as was the Amish way. That told Jack that Grace Miller could be bought.

And she needed those horses alive.

When no more gunshots went off, Jack wondered if that was the proof he needed to show she had teamed up with this operation. But she knew the thoroughbred had been moved to the trailer. So why was she putting her life at risk for the other horses?

Was he wrong about her?

THREE

Grace had her *halsduch* cape unpinned and pulled over her head before she reached the open barn doors. Flames flickered outward, but she could see there was still room for her to slip inside. Knowing that the shooter was somewhere outside encouraged her to race forward to get out of the line of *that* fire, too. As she drew closer and closer, she expected to hear another shot go off, stopping her from rescuing her horses before the flames grew too fierce.

Heavy footsteps thudded behind her. Before she could turn her head, Jack Kaufman ran up beside her and wrapped an arm around her shoulders. "Stay low!" he yelled, pulling her closer to shield her the rest of the way to the barn.

They reached the doors and, with faces turned away from the flames, ran inside.

"Grab the blanket on the hook," she yelled, while she threw her heavy organdy cape over the flame closest to the first stall to stomp it out.

The FBI agent lifted the blanket and threw it over

the strongest blaze. Together they beat at the fire until it was finally out.

Grace's heart raced, and her breathing was fast and rasping. "The shooter must have struck a lantern and knocked it into the hay," she said, feeling her adrenaline slowly start to ebb.

"That was my fault," the agent said, taking his cap off and swiping at his forehead. "I lit the lantern and left it on when I went to your door."

Grace took in the smoldering hay scattered across the dirt floor. A slow awareness of pain radiated up her legs. As she began to squirm, she said, "And I threw the hay down to try and catch my thief. It made for a fire hazard that didn't have to…"

She couldn't say another word as agony overcame her, emanating from her feet.

Her bare feet.

She hadn't thought her actions through before racing to put the fire out.

Grace stumbled back, and as she raised her head she caught the lawman staring at her. She watched shock overtake his face and knew it had to match her own.

In an instant, he dropped his hat and stepped in front of her, then swept her up in his arms.

"Put me down!" she tried to yell, but her voice cracked with pain.

"You foolish woman," he muttered. At this close range, and without the black cap, she could see his temple pulsing. He fixed his gaze on the house, and she knew there was nothing she could say to stop him, even if she could speak through the growing burn. With her in his arms, the lawman raced forward. "What were you thinking? And I don't just mean about your bare feet and the fire. These people are not to be messed with. Why would you ever deal with them?"

As if on cue, a shot rang out from the trees. The lawman grunted, but kept running, now bending his head to cover her as much as possible. He reached the porch steps, taking two at a time, just as another shot sounded. The bullet pelted the floorboards at his feet, missing its mark.

The door swung wide, and he carried her through. Her father had opened it for them this time, but he shrank and cowered back when the lawman kicked it shut again.

He lowered her to the floor instantly. "Stay down," he ordered, then looked up at her father. Grace expected him to bark orders at her *daed* as he had with her, but he surprised her with a quiet tone. "Benjamin, I'm going to sit you on the floor. It is safer there." He handled the elderly man gently, his strong hands guiding him down beside her.

Grace watched the lawman crawl to a window, his gun back in his hand and at the ready to shoot. The sight stupefied her. How had such an event come to be? This farmhouse had been the only home she'd ever known and had always been filled with peace and laughter, even after her *mamm* died. Grace did her best to put aside her grief, making sure her *daed* received what he needed as his mind deteriorated further. Benjamin Miller was a wonderful father—even if most days now he didn't remember he had a child.

"It's been quiet since we got inside," Grace said in a timid voice at last. "Do you think he's gone?"

"If he is, it won't be for long. He came for the horse. He can't go back empty-handed." The daunting Jack Kaufman glanced her way, his expression skeptical. "As I'm sure you know."

Grace shook her head in denial, then gave up with a sigh. What else could she say? Nothing. "Think what you want about me. I know the truth."

"And that would be what?" His right eyebrow arched. "Let's hear it. And I only want the truth. Nothing else."

Grace pressed her lips tight, not wanting to tell this bullish man anything. He'd done nothing but invade her life and home, treating her like a criminal ever since he'd showed up with his gun drawn on her.

But to say nothing in self-defense could land her in handcuffs.

With her mind made up, she laid out the facts. "I'm the horse trader's daughter. I've been helping my father with the dealings for as long as I can remember. It's all I know." Grace frowned, glancing at her *daed.* "And now…it's up to me to take over the business—"

"Your bishop will allow that?" Agent Kaufman interrupted.

The air whooshed from Grace's lungs. How did he know what to say to trip her up?

He wanted the truth, but to tell him Bishop Bontrager would be receptive to her taking the reins from her father would be a lie. The elder had already made it clear he had someone in mind to take over the business when Benjamin was no longer up to the task.

Grace reached for her father's weakened hand. Squeezing it, she searched his eyes to see if he recognized her. His smile calmed her enough to continue. Her *daed* was beside her, giving her all she needed to impart the rest of the details to the agent.

"I will lose my job," she admitted, looking around the room. "And all you see here. The horse trader is supposed to be a man. It's not right for a woman to be dealing with such things."

"You say that like you've memorized the rules, but don't actually believe them."

Grace searched his face. Again, the man saw too much. "It's been three months since I started going alone to the racetrack in my father's place," she admitted, instead of replying to his comment. "I've handled it competently. I meant for Bishop Bontrager to see my father taught me well."

"Did your father teach you to steal?"

"No. Of course not. He taught me what to look for in a good buggy horse. He taught me how to place a bid on the horses that the track rejected for racing. Just because they aren't fast enough for harness racing doesn't mean they should be put to pasture. The Amish live a slow life. We don't need fast horses."

"I know all about the slow life."

Grace squinted up at him, not sure how the man knew about her way of life. "You've interrogated other Amish people before?"

He suppressed a laugh and looked out the window from the edge of the curtain, not responding.

What did she expect? He was here for answers, not questions.

"Go on," he instructed, as he dropped the curtain and moved away from the window. He placed his gun in its holster and walked to the basin and water pump in the kitchen. He cranked the handle with ease, then brought the full basin back into the living room. "I said go on."

But Grace could only stare at him, wondering what he planned to do with the water. Until he knelt in front of her and reached for one of her ankles.

She jerked her leg back. "No. You don't have to do that."

"You just keep talking. I can't be bringing my prisoner in with burned feet. My boss won't take too kindly to that." He pressed a cool, wet rag to the scorched sole.

Grace inhaled sharply at the contact. She sighed as relief took over.

Then his words propelled her to finish her side of the story. She couldn't be taken anywhere, never mind prison. Her father needed her to keep things going at home.

"I go to Autumn Woods every Tuesday and Saturday when they are testing their horses, and sit in the stands. When one fails the trainers' tests, they look to the bidders and ask if anyone wants to buy it. I raise my hand when I see a horse that would be a good fit for the Amish. Like I said, my father taught me well. I know when to bid and when not to. They give me a ticket for each horse I buy, and I take them to the stables when I am ready to leave. I hand over the tickets, and they tie up my horses behind my buggy. That's it."

"What price did you pay for the horse today?"

Grace nodded at the desk across the room. "Twelve hundred. The papers are in the drawer. You're welcome to look at them. You'll see I paid a fair price for each one. I didn't steal those horses."

Jack reached into a pocket on his pant leg. He took out a sheet of paper and showed her a list of numbers. "These are the identification codes of some of the stolen horses. These are the codes for thoroughbreds, not standardbreds. They are tattooed on the horses' inner upper lip."

"I know all about the identifications. A thoroughbred begins with the letter of the year of its foaling, followed by four or five numbers."

"So you know a look when we go out there will prove one way or the other if any of those are the stolen horses, but I'll save you the suspense. I already checked."

"And?"

"And I wouldn't still be here if you weren't my thief."

Jack felt Grace stiffen under his touch. She was burned, but he knew her response had less to do with his ministrations and more to do with his accusation. He took the next foot and examined it. "This one looks better than the other. You must stomp heavier with your right foot. Ever thought of taking up square dancing?" He tried to lighten the mood, but his attempt at a joke fell flat. He wrapped the foot in the cool cloth and pressed gently. "Sorry, I forgot the Amish don't dance. But we do sing."

"We?"

Jack winced at his slip. "Old news. I grew up in a community in Colorado. I left eight years ago, when I was eighteen. End of story."

"That hardly sounds like the end of that story."

Jack shrugged and locked his gaze on Grace's wide eyes. So inquisitive for the Amish, but then, Grace was unique all around. She was a fighter, and that in itself was as unlike the Amish as could be.

Jack recollected his first glimpse of her in the barn, her pitchfork held high. He had to bite down on the inside of his cheek to keep from smiling. She might think he was trying to make light of the situation again, and this really was no time to laugh about anything. Not when he was going to have to arrest her.

"You have stolen goods on your property, or at least one of them," he said, bringing the subject back to her. "You've told me your story, but it doesn't explain how you ended up with a thoroughbred, instead of the standardbred you purchased."

"Th-thoroughbred?" She swallowed hard as her eyes filled with shock. Or most likely feigned shock. "H-how?" Her voice cracked.

Jack bit back a smile. Even if she was faking it he found the sight of her bewilderment endearing. He could almost believe she was innocent in all this. Almost. "That's what I've been asking you to explain. How did you switch the horse today without the stable hands not noticing?"

Grace reached for the papers with the identification codes. As she silently read them her eyes grew wide in shock. "These *are* thoroughbred numbers. I can't believe this. I didn't even look at the identifications. I've just been concerned with showing the bishop I could handle the job." She glanced toward the door and moved to stand up.

"Whoa," Jack said, keeping her down with a hand on her shoulder. "I'll need to clear the woods before you go anywhere tonight."

"I have to protect that horse until I can get him back to the stables. Do you have any idea what a thoroughbred is worth? They are purebred."

"I've done my research, yes."

Her face blanched further. "I've already lost two horses to the thief. What if..." Her eyes searched his with growing fear. Shaking her head, she said, "I can't replace them or pay for them."

"I gathered that," he said.

"You don't understand." Panic made her hands shake as she reached for his, still holding her foot. "I could go to jail."

Jack nodded. "That's what I've been saying, *ya*." He cringed at his unconscious slip into the old language. One night with this woman, and his past was already breaching the borders of his new life. He looked to see if Grace had caught his dialect, but she was facing her father.

Benjamin slumped back against the wall, watching them talk with a look of confusion on his face. "Oh, *Daed*. What should I do?" she implored him.

Benjamin squinted in response. If he had an answer, he wasn't sharing it with his daughter.

For the first time since Jack met Grace tonight, he saw tears well up in her eyes. Not even when she was being shot at did she cry. But in this moment, with her father unreachable, he could see how much Grace relied on him.

With Benjamin inaccessible, she was left to take

care of everything alone. Left to run the business as perfectly as possible, so the elders wouldn't take her job away from her.

Signing on with a horse theft ring wouldn't be the way she would go, not if she wants to show how well she can handle the job.

The thought bounced around in Jack's head—and disrupted his plan.

The plan was to bring in his horse thief, no matter what.

But what if I'm wrong?

The idea seemed ludicrous. He was never wrong. He always had a way of sizing a person up and knowing if he had his man…or woman, as the case may be. That talent traced all the way back to Colorado, when someone had pinned a crime on him. He'd figured out who was behind the scheme and had called him out—even if he'd had to stand alone to do it.

But that was another story.

After that day, Jack had vowed he would always seek justice, and he wouldn't stop until he had the right criminal behind bars. Up until this point he hadn't been wrong when he'd brought a perpetrator in.

Could he be wrong about Grace?

Jack studied her crestfallen face as she searched her father's confused gaze. Jack wasn't ready to give in and admit to being wrong about her. Too much evidence was stacked against her. She'd had the stolen horse in her barn…and now in his trailer.

But maybe…

Jack pressed his lips together in annoyance. He typically liked a good joke, but not when the joke was on him. He could imagine his supervisor, Nic Harrington, laughing hysterically if Jack brought in an Amish woman who was completely innocent. Nic would never let him live it down.

Before Jack could slap cuffs on anyone, he would need to be 100 percent sure he had the right person.

But first, he had to catch the gunman in the trees.

Jack winced as he stood up to go. He'd hidden from Grace the fact that the gunman had clipped him. Something that the man would pay dearly for.

"I'll tell you what you're going to do," he responded, when Grace's question to her father went unanswered. He opened the door. "You're going to prove your innocence."

"How will I do that?" she asked, clearly bewildered as she looked up at him from the floor.

"I'm going with you to Autumn Woods."

Her eyes widened once again. "But what will I say when I'm asked why I'm with an Englisher?"

"You won't be." At her confusion, he said, "I'm going to need some of your *daed*'s clothes."

"You're going to pretend to be Amish? I don't like this at all."

"*Ya*, me neither. But believe me, this is going to hurt me so much more than it will hurt you."

Just then the sound of a vehicle starting up outside alerted Jack to the present danger. *How?* He felt for his keys in his pocket.

"That's your truck. With my horse!" Grace shouted. She jumped to her feet, then crumpled back to the floor in obvious pain, clearly not going anywhere.

Jack withdrew the keys from his pocket, needing to

get outside. But instead of reaching for the doorknob, he stepped forward to help Grace. Instantly, she waved him away, struggling to speak through the pain. Then she forced out the only word he needed to hear.

"Go!"

FOUR

Grace released the pent-up breath she'd been holding since Jack left, slamming the door behind him. She stretched out her throbbing feet and winced from her burns. Her days of walking *barr fees* were over much earlier in the season than normal. Autumn was only beginning, and she should have had a few more weeks of warm weather to walk the farm with no shoes.

Two gunshots echoed through the night, reminding her of the danger just outside her front door. Both she and her *daed* jolted in their places on the floor. Her lack of shoes was the least of her worries when there was a gunman on the loose.

"Are we under attack?" Grace's father laid his forehead on her shoulder. His voice had never sounded so fearful. The whole scenario was unfathomable for their simple Amish lifestyle, never mind for someone whose mind couldn't comprehend normal, everyday things.

As Grace rubbed his cheek, she looked up at the closed door. The FBI agent had just left through it, hoping to catch the thief stealing his truck and trailer—*and* her horse. Would she hear another gunshot? Or had the thief just found his mark?

"I wish I could say no, *Daed*, but I'm not sure what's going on. It appears someone is using me to steal horses from Autumn Woods, and the FBI believe I'm involved." Grace wasn't sure how much of that her father understood, if anything. She didn't understand it herself. "What do I do? I could be in a lot of trouble."

"We mustn't fight," he said solemnly, and lifted his head. "No *fechde*."

Grace frowned at his appropriate reply. It was not what she wanted to hear. His Amish gentleness stayed true, even when he could lose his daughter to prison. He didn't understand what was at stake. But he was still right. There could be no fighting.

"I know," she replied, and swallowed a growing lump of resentment. With the possibility of going to jail, Grace wondered how far God would ask her to go.

She thought of Joseph in the Old Testament, wrongly accused of a crime that had put him in jail for years. As horrifying as it was for him, Joseph had to go there to save many lives. God needed him there. God's will was done. "*Gött*'s will be done to me, as well," she said under her breath. Her gaze dropped to her folded hands in her lap. A prayer formed in her heart, and she spoke it quietly as her eyes drifted closed. She sought protection for herself and her father in whatever place they were called to go from here.

Grace opened her eyes and lifted her gaze to the window the agent had been standing by earlier. The curtain billowed out in the slight breeze. Then Grace heard the truck's engine shut down. Someone was out there.

Was it the agent? Or the thief?

Rising up on her knees, Grace crawled over to the window, careful to keep her skirt under her, protecting her from the broken glass. As she reached the window, she noticed a stain on her white curtains. Smudges of dirt, she thought.

But when she touched the fabric, a bit of the substance came off on her fingers. She studied her fingertips, then looked at the floor in front of her, finding little droplets of a dark liquid.

Grace dabbed her pointer finger in one and knew in an instant what it was.

"He's bleeding," she whispered, as the possibility became real.

Agent Kaufman was injured. *But how?*

It didn't matter.

"*Daed*, he's hurt!" Grace spoke louder, crawling back to her father. She pushed herself up on her feet, then cried out, crumpling back to the floor in pain.

Carefully moving to stand on the edges of her feet, Grace found her balance and caught her breath. "*Daed*, I have to go outside. The agent is bleeding."

Grace remembered the grunt the lawman had given when he was carrying her. Had he been shot and never said a thing?

She glanced to the floor where he had placed her and taken care of her burned feet. He had lowered her father so gently, as well, all the while hurt and bleeding from his own wound?

The idea bewildered her. It was a gesture of charity

even in the midst of pain. And now he was out there searching for the gunman.

Or bleeding out.

Grace felt at an impasse. Should she go out to look for him and help him? Or stay inside and risk him never returning?

Whatever she chose would put them in danger. But if she stayed inside, she would invite the danger in.

Grace's eyes filled with tears at her father's feebleness. Whatever she did, she had to make sure he was safe. That's all that mattered.

"*Daed*, I'm going to go out for a while. I'll be back real soon," she said, in the most normal voice she could muster.

Benjamin squinted up at her and she knew he wasn't placing her. She figured it was just as well. In a sad way, his brain was protecting him through this ordeal. When this nightmare was over, hopefully he wouldn't remember a single gunshot.

Though Agent Kaufman would.

Grace limped over to the closet and found a pair of her father's boots. She bound wet rags around her feet and gingerly slipped them into the boots. A careful test proved she could endure walking in them. At the door, she reached for a lantern to take with her, but thought better of it. A flame would only draw attention. Still, going out empty-handed seemed just as dangerous.

An idea flickered in her mind, one that seemed so wrong.

A glance in the direction of the closet, with its door still opened wide, showed her the long box with the shotgun was still there. She'd never fired it but had seen her *daed* load it enough times to understand the mechanics involved.

She looked his way, and it was as though her father could read her thoughts. His head tilted, and his green eyes sought hers for an excuse valid enough to go against the Amish way of no violence.

She had none.

With quiet acceptance, she opened the door and walked out into the dark of night empty-handed. She couldn't use a weapon to help the agent, but Grace didn't think there were any rules about creating a diversion.

She looked to the barn and the trailer. The thoroughbred kicked up a fuss against the steel sides. Grace headed toward the horses and thought that she just might have the perfect weapon, or weapons.

Three to be exact.

As soon as Jack left Grace's house, he shot his truck's tire to stop the thief from riding out with the vehicle and trailer. With a flat tire, the pickup couldn't go anywhere, but by the time Jack made it there the driver's side door was open and the cab was empty. The man had run off.

Jack scanned the tree line, knowing he would have to go in if he was going to catch this guy. The horse thief wasn't leaving without the thoroughbred, and Jack wasn't leaving without his thief—or thieves, if Grace Miller was really part of the operation. Although that was appearing to be not the case, he wouldn't rule it out yet, especially since he'd witnessed her taking the horse at the track.

Jack reached under the dashboard and pulled apart the twisted strands that had hotwired the vehicle. With the engine killed and his gun up, he headed toward the base of the cliff for a game of cat and mouse in the woods.

Jack held his weapon in his right hand. His other palm was pressed tightly against his left side, where a bullet had clipped him during his run with Grace. "Thank you, God," he muttered under his breath. The gash burned like crazy, but could have been so much worse than a missing chunk of skin. It still could be dangerous if he didn't stop the bleeding, of course. Judging by the feel of the wound, the gunman had nothing bigger than a .22. Most likely why he'd missed his mark from out in the woods.

Jack pulled his hand away, only to find fresh blood on it. Well, maybe it wasn't a complete miss. But at least the bullet didn't get Grace. At least she was still locked up safely in her home. Jack would play hide-and-seek with this gunman all night if it meant keeping him away from Grace and Benjamin.

Jack pressed his hand over his side again and tilted an ear to his right. The sounds of leaves rustling in the breeze mingled with a few far-off crickets. Then he heard what he was waiting for.

The snap of a twig.

The gunman was off to his right, just as Jack had predicted. Moving stealthily, he followed the other sounds the thief made, and soon realized the guy wasn't very smart. So far, he had moved in the same right, right, left pattern. Jack figured it was so he could find his way out of the forest. But that also meant he could be tracked.

And just like that, Jack became the stalker with the upper hand.

He readied his gun as he took silent steps to his right. At ten feet, he turned left to keep to the gunman's right. Jack picked up his pace to outmatch his target's. He took one more turn, this time left, and came face-to-face with a shadowed figure in the dark, his eyes wild at being caught.

"Who are you?" Jack asked into the night, his trigger finger ready to pull. He stepped closer and noticed a bandana covered half the man's face.

Or more like a boy's.

Jack huffed in disbelief. "They're hiring them younger and younger these days. How old are you? Seventeen?"

"None of your business. I'm here for the horse, but you have inconvenienced me."

Jack laughed aloud. "That's a big word for such a little guy. That's a good one." He laughed again.

The gunman's eyes narrowed with anger. "How would you like another bullet in you?"

Jack's laughter stopped cold. "I let you take a shot at me once. It won't happen again."

The boy lifted his gun straight at Jack's head. Jack wasn't about to give him another chance to fire.

He jerked to the right as his left hand reached for the gun and pushed it away. The weapon blasted, but the boy gripped it firmly as they grappled together.

The sound of a horse running interrupted them. Then Jack heard the thud of several horses' hooves on the hard ground.

"There's more than one," he said aloud.

"The horses!" the boy yelled frantically. "The horses are loose!" He took off in the direction of one of the running animals, then veered to go after another. "Which one is it?"

Jack could see the boy knew what was at stake if he didn't return with the thoroughbred.

His life.

"Tell me who you work for, and I can help you," Jack said. He hadn't moved from his spot, just turned to watch the boy grow more and more frustrated.

"She did this!" the boy wildly yelled. "I knew she would be trouble. I knew it wouldn't be that easy."

"You think the Amish woman did this?" Jack asked, biting back an amused laugh at the idea. Then he gave the remark some thought. The boy had to be right. Only Grace could have released the horses and caused the confusion.

But that wasn't all she'd managed to do.

"That little Amish woman not only freed the horses, but she managed to disarm you," he said with a smirk.

The boy looked down at his hands, now empty. He lifted confused eyes and saw two guns now in Jack's possession. The boy's own gun was now aimed at him.

"So tell me who you are," Jack ordered.

The boy's eyes flitted from side to side before resting on Jack. Slowly, he peered through angry eyes. "I've got all night. How long do you have before you bleed out?" He lifted his head in defiance.

Jack recognized that smug expression. He'd been just a little bit older when he had given that same look to his family and walked away forever. Only Jack had gone into law enforcement. This kid wouldn't make it out of his teens if he stayed on a track of crime much longer.

"You're a dead man," Jack said. "You know that, right? And it won't be me pulling the trigger that does you in."

"That only means I've got nothing to lose."

Jack shook his head. "You've got everything to lose. You're just too blind to see it right now. Let me help you."

A crunch of leaves to Jack's left alerted them to the presence of someone else. Jack expected to see a horse trotting in, but at the silhouette of an Amish woman, he knew it was Grace. His weakening state held him back a fraction of a second too long. Just the time the boy needed to reach down to his ankle, then spring into a run at Grace. He wrapped an arm around her neck just as Jack leaped toward them.

Grace shrieked and flailed. Quickly, her body stilled, and she whimpered.

Jack rushed the last few steps until he realized the boy had a knife to her throat. It must have been strapped to his ankle, Jack thought distractedly, while his brain raced to figure out his next move.

He raised his hands in surrender. "I'm not going to shoot you. I only want to help you get away from these people before it's too late for you." He set the guns at his feet to show his words rang true.

But he readied himself to spring in and take the boy down.

"You forgot one thing," the youth said, keeping Grace's back pressed tightly against him. "I don't want to get away. I was going places. And this is so much bigger than a few horses."

Grace struggled to get free and cried out again when her assailant twisted her arm. She was yelling as Jack took another slow step forward. He was nearly there when he saw her lift her right foot and jam it down hard on the boy's instep. He noticed she wore large boots now just as the boy hollered out in pain, and she did the same.

The young thief let go of her, and she fell to the ground. Boots forgotten, Jack took the opportunity to run at the boy, but just as he was about to make contact, his opponent turned and ran into the dark.

Jack started to go after him, but knew that in his current state he'd never catch up. Still, he had to try.

Then he heard Grace crying behind him.

Jack stopped where he stood, torn in two directions.

But he couldn't leave Grace sobbing.

"Are you hurt?" he asked, retracing his steps to her. "Did he cut you? Or is it your foot? I saw you stomp on him. With your burns that took some guts."

Grace lifted her face to him. Fear shone in her widened eyes. "I fought back," she whispered in despair.

Jack grabbed his side with a grunt as he knelt to face her. He frowned at seeing her agony, both physical and emotional, then sighed and helped her to her feet. Automatically, they leaned together for support. "I know you think you fought back, Grace, but actually, you saved his life. For at least tonight. I was going to have to take him down."

"But he's only a boy."

"It was either you or him, and trust me, it wouldn't have been you."

Her face lifted to his. So close, he could feel her soft breath on his chin. He studied her bewildered expression and knew before she said a word what she would have had him do. He knew the Amish way of turning the other cheek. "In my line of business, I do my best to avoid bloodshed, but if there must be some, I aim for the one who's holding the weapon, not for the innocent bystander caught in the fray."

"Like yourself?" she asked, her gaze locked on his. "I know you were shot. I found your blood in my home."

Jack didn't deny it. With a shrug, he said, "I'll live. It's just a graze."

"We still need to tend to the wound. It could become infected." The angle of her chin told him she wouldn't take no for an answer.

"I thought Amish women were supposed to be passive," he grumbled.

"I'll take that as the pain talking."

Jack bit back a grin. She was different from the Amish women he'd grown up with. Maybe she would have stuck up for him when he was younger, even when his family hadn't.

No, probably not.

He let the wishful thinking go and said, "First we need to round up the horses. They're my first priority."

"Not me anymore? Does this mean you believe I'm innocent now?" Hope brightened her eyes.

Jack paused before answering. The image of Grace

tying the stolen horse to her buggy was fixed in his mind. "It's not my job to determine your innocence."

"But—"

"Let's go. Our shooter could return at any second with backup." He took her elbow to guide her out of the woods.

"But do you still think I'm guilty?" she asked as they moved gingerly through the trees. If her feet were paining her, she didn't mention it. He'd give her points for that.

But he still avoided her question. "Tomorrow, you're taking me to the track, and you're going to show me what you do there. Cooperate with me, and I might put in a good word to my supervisor."

They left the woods, but before they descended the hill toward the house, Grace clicked her tongue, and two horses came stomping up behind them. They approached her and stood by, panting and nickering, and nosing her outstretched hand.

She had a gentle way with horses that Jack found sweet.

But not enough to make him walk away.

"I'll round up the other horse," he said. "Before he's long gone."

"Please do find him." Grace worried her lower lip. "I don't want another animal in these people's hands. I won't let it happen. And I need to get the others back from them. It sounds like they've been doing this for a while."

"How do you plan to do that? Do you know who the kid's boss is?"

"No, but I'll be ready when he comes back." She took slow steps, almost hobbling toward the house.

Jack hurried to take her arm again. "You don't get it. Horse thefts are big business. If the boss thinks you can identify him, he will make sure you never do. You're not safe here. Especially with the boy. In fact, he's more dangerous than ever now because you embarrassed him by making him lose his gun. You won't be safe until I know who he's working for."

"How will you find out?"

"I don't know yet, but at least I know one thing beyond a reasonable doubt."

"What's that?"

"Innocent or not, the danger has only begun for you. And it's nothing you can be ready for."

FIVE

From her upstairs bedroom window, Grace watched the sun rise over the cliff behind her home. Her head had never hit the pillow all night, and she still wore her blue dress from the day before. A glance down to the truck showed Agent Kaufman changing a tire. They hadn't said a word to each other since they'd come back to the house. She'd asked about caring for his gunshot wound, but he quickly refused her aid and left to retrieve the thoroughbred.

A thoroughbred.

Such a liability for her, especially during these times with her *daed*. But then, so was having an English FBI agent on the property. How would she explain either of these scenarios to the bishop and elders? With each passing day, she lost a little more of her grasp on the farm.

Agent Kaufman had told her to leave out some of her father's clothes, but even though she chose articles from her *daed*'s younger, more robust days, they still wouldn't make the English man look Amish. Everyone would be able to tell, and that would lead to more trouble for her. It was no wonder she couldn't think of sleeping. When so much turmoil hung in the balance, sleep would have to wait.

The truck started, the sound of its engine startling her from her reverie. Jack was now behind the wheel.

Was he leaving?

Grace leaned forward in her chair to watch the truck and horse trailer drive up to the barn. The agent didn't turn and head down the driveway toward the road, but instead pulled around the outbuildings and past the cornfields, heading to the cliff. From the window, the truck remained in view until it reached the trees and disappeared.

Grace stood, intending to run from the room, but immediately whimpered in pain and fell back into her chair. She bit her lower lip as she breathed through the burning ache on the soles of her feet. Even with the salve she'd lathered on, they would take time to heal. Grace decided to wrap them again with clean bandages, to allow for protection and padding. Her father's boots were still beside her bed, and with them back on, she gave it another attempt, this time walking slowly and cautiously.

She padded out into the hall and down the stairs just in time to hear the closing of a car door. She made her way to the front door and opened it, expecting to see that the agent had returned.

But it wasn't a truck in her driveway.

"Good morning, Grace. Sorry to come by so early." Sheriff Hank Maddox walked up the steps to the porch. He removed his brimmed hat and held it in front of him with both hands. His hairline receded more and more as he approached his sixties, and beneath his forehead, he wore big sunglasses, even though the morning sun wasn't burning brightly just yet. "I got a call from a neighbor who was concerned about some possible gunfire they heard a few hours ago. Have you had any trouble out here?" He leaned to the right to look behind her into the house.

Grace's attention moved from him to his police cruiser, then over to the tree line where the agent had gone. With no sign of him, she answered, "Yes, Sheriff, the horse thief returned last night, and he shot off a gun."

Sheriff Maddox pressed his lips into a tight line. "I don't like the sound of that, Grace. I want you to consider installing a phone in the barn. If guns are involved, then this thief is not Amish as you thought. I want you to be able to call me at a moment's notice. I do hope no one was hurt."

Grace curled her sore toes. She also thought of Agent Kaufman's bullet injury.

Before she could respond, Hank Maddox stepped close and put a black boot over the threshold. "This has crossed a dangerous line. You can't be naive, Grace. This is serious."

Grace ran her gaze up his large frame, then locked it on the reflection of herself in his lenses. She hated that she saw fear staring back at her. But she also hated to lie to the sheriff, even if Hank had proved to her that word wouldn't get back to the bishop. Lying would be wrong.

"I've told you before, it's nothing that I can't handle," she said. "I really don't need you to concern yourself with this." She swallowed hard before saying, "Or with me. I appreciate all you have done for me these past few months since *Mamm*'s death. Your understanding of our ways of living life out of the spotlight and the news has been appreciated, but I can handle this problem." The sheriff had been able to keep a buggy accident out of the news, but there was no way he would be able to keep a thoroughbred theft and shootout from making headlines.

Hank stood still for a moment. Then he removed his glasses with one hand. His light blue eyes held a look of affection. She'd seen it more and more these days, but always acted like she didn't. "With your *mamm*'s passing and your *daed*'s illness, I know your days are hard. I can't pretend to not care. You're like a daughter to me. Please consider me a friend. Things are only going to get harder with your father. It will be good to know you have people to reach out to for help."

Grace sighed and smiled up at the man, who was at least thirty years her senior. She was being silly by ignoring his act of friendship, even if he was English.

"I'm sorry, Sheriff—"

"Hank," he corrected, like he always did.

Grace frowned. She didn't feel right using his name in a personal way. "You know the Amish don't affiliate with the law. We are supposed to handle problems on our own, in our own way. Accepting your help is hard for me."

"And just how are you handling these thefts?" he asked.

Before she answered, she heard a throat being cleared behind her, followed by a man's heavy footsteps. Too heavy to be her *daed*.

"*I'm* here to help the Millers," a deep voice said. "I came right away when I heard there was a trouble-maker."

Grace glanced out of the corner of her eye to see a tall Amish man. For a moment, she didn't know who stood beside her. But in a flash, the realization of his identity had her turning to openly gawk.

A transformed Jack Kaufman tapped his chin to tell her to close her mouth.

He told the sheriff his name, but Grace didn't hear much after that as she studied every minute detail of his attire. The changes went beyond the clothing she'd left out for him. His hair reached the correct length beneath his black brimmed hat. It had to be fake. How else could it have grown so fast?

But that wasn't all that was fake.

The way Jack stood was not his normal authoritative body language. Instead, the lanky man towering over her projected a humble demeanor. His shoulders drooped and his chin stayed low as he addressed Sheriff Maddox.

Hank smirked in a condescending way. "If you don't mind me asking, what makes you think you can hold off a man with a gun?"

Jack was slow to respond as he lifted a hand to rub his clean-shaven face, now so smooth. Grace didn't know what made her reenter the conversation. Maybe it was Jack's transformation into a credible Amish man, or maybe it was Hank's sudden conceit, but she straightened to her full five-feet height, looped an arm through Jack's and stepped close to him.

"Jack is a family friend from a community in upstate

New York. They do a lot of hunting and are good with a gun. He makes his targets practically with his eyes closed. That gunman last night won't be back, that I am certain sure of. Right, Jack?" She pulled on his arm, and her chipper voice hung between them.

The dark brown eyes Jack leveled on her told her to stop while she was ahead. "If he does, we'll be sure to let you know, Sheriff." Jack turned to Hank and held out a hand to shake. "Thank you for checking in on Grace and Benjamin. I really appreciate it."

At first Hank didn't take the proffered hand, but then he reached out and slowly nodded. "I'm glad to hear you have some sense." Hank glanced Grace's way, then he asked, "How long do you plan to stay, Jack? Just so I know when Grace might need some help."

Grace felt Jack tense beside her. He said, "I'm able to stay as long as I need to."

Hank stepped back. He put his sunglasses back on and patted his Stetson. "Just don't go taking the law into your hands, or these matters won't be your own anymore. I will have to get involved." He looked Grace's way, and with a warning nod, headed down the steps and back to his cruiser. His tires spit gravel behind them as he headed down the driveway and out onto the road.

It wasn't until his car disappeared from sight that Grace and Jack uttered a single word, simultaneously.

"*Ach*."

"Amos, you came." Benjamin raced into the living room and reached out to Jack. He let the old man hold him tight as he looked over his shoulder at Grace's startled expression. Then he mouthed, *"Who is Amos?"*

"*Daed*'s little brother." She lifted her hands in a helpless gesture. "He must think you're him." Grace put her hands on Benjamin's shoulders. "*Daed*, this isn't—"

Jack shook his head to stop her. He patted Benjamin's back. "It's all right, *brudder. Ich bin doh.*" Jack asked about Benjamin's state of well-being.

"We had an intruder last night!" the elderly man confided, mentioning his frantic fears the night before.

Grace frowned and tears filled her eyes, which were greener than Jack had realized. In the shadowy darkness the night before he'd thought they looked blue. But now the liquid bluish-green hue reminded him of a wooded pool in the Sangre de Cristo Mountains of Colorado where he used to swim. But those memories had turned nightmarish the day his hands were put in handcuffs, just as Grace's eyes did for her father's frightened mind.

"All is well," Jack said to both of them. "I promise to catch him."

Benjamin shook his head and spoke at a rapid rate. "*Ar mawg 'n deeb si, oddar 'n marder.*" He lifted his head and with piercing eyes, searched Jack's face. Would Benjamin realize that Jack was not Amos? Jack braced for the accusation, but then Benjamin repeated the dreaded words for thief and murderer. "*Deeb* and *Marder.*" Fearful tears sprung to his old eyes.

The idea of a thieving murderer on the loose was no joking matter. The man had a valid reason for being afraid. Especially when he couldn't protect his daughter. Jack leaned close, peering into the old man's eyes.

"I will protect you."

"*Fershprech*?" Benjamin implored Jack for reassurance.

"I promise." Jack looked past Benjamin and studied Grace's worried look as she bit her lower lip. Just a few hours ago, he had come here to arrest her. He still might have to, but for now he could relieve their fears of danger. As long as he was there, they would be safe. "I promise," he said to her, drawing her attention away from her father.

Her body visibly relaxed before him. She sighed and her shoulders fell, as did her eyelids. She reached for Benjamin's hand. "*Komm.* It's time for breakfast."

Jack watched the two of them slowly make their way toward the kitchen. He might be making a big mistake protecting her, but until he had more information from the racetrack, he would hold off detaining her. To bring her in and find out later he'd been wrong wouldn't look good for him. But if he was right, and she was involved…

Jack shook his head. He would do the right thing and bring her in if that turned out to be the case. Regardless of her pretty eyes, he would do his job.

The smell of eggs and bacon quickly filled the house, and Jack's stomach growled. He was so hungry he could eat a *gaul*. A horse.

A silent laugh escaped his lips at the irony. All this danger had befallen Grace because of stolen horseflesh. People would go to great lengths for a good horse. Even become thieves and murderers.

But why? There had to be a good reason to go that far.

Jack closed the front door and walked to the kitchen.

He took in the interaction between the daughter and her ailing father. If Grace was involved, he knew why. She would have convinced herself Benjamin was worth the risk. That he would need more resources for his care than she alone could provide.

But that didn't explain the people in charge of the operation. They would have very different reasons. Ones much more sinister.

A sound from outside caught his attention while he helped set the table for the food Grace was preparing. Jack stepped to the window and noticed a horse and buggy coming up the driveway.

"Visitors," he said.

Grace hobbled over to the window with a plate in her hand and moved the curtain aside. Instantly, the plate slipped from her fingers and shattered into pieces across the floor.

She shrieked at the sound, but looked frantically from the window to Jack. Whoever was out there had her green eyes darkening to blue again and had rendered her unable to speak.

"I take it this isn't a friendly visit," he said.

Grace shook her head. "Two days in a row I will have to fight for my life."

He patted his side. "Shall I get my gun out?"

She huffed. "I don't typically like guns, but for this visit, keep it close."

SIX

The slow thunk of heavy footsteps on the stairs outside the kitchen paralyzed Grace, gluing her to her spot by the window. Any decision to be made seemed out of her reach and impossible. Should she hide Agent Kaufman? Should she hide her father? Should she hide herself?

None of those things were going to happen. Grace resigned herself to the inevitable. Deep down, she'd always known things couldn't go on much longer.

But she had hoped…

The knock came on the door.

"Are you going to answer it?" Agent Kaufman asked. "Or do you want me to?"

"I should be the one," she said nervously. "Have a seat with *Daed* and serve your breakfast. I'll invite them in."

Once Jack did as she asked, Grace braced herself with a deep breath and smoothed her apron. She opened the door wide.

"Bishop Bontrager, what a nice—" The rest of Grace's greeting lodged in her throat when she noticed Thomas Bontrager hadn't come alone. She cleared her throat. "—surprise. I see you brought Leroy Mast with you. I'm sorry, I wasn't expecting you." Grace stepped back and waved them in. "Please, *komm.* We are just having breakfast. I hope you can join us."

The bishop stepped over the threshold without a word. His tall frame filled the doorway, and he removed his hat, the extra wide brim of which denoted his high stature within the community. Patting down his stark white hair, he waited for Leroy to follow him before turning toward the kitchen table.

Grace held her breath, waiting for him to ask who the Amish man at the table was. But her father stood up and spoke first. Jack reached to stop him, but even touching his arm didn't keep *Daed*'s mouth closed.

"I have a visitor. Amos has come to help me with the business. Isn't that *wunderbar*?"

Thomas glanced Leroy's way with a shocked expression on his bearded face. "*Ya*, that is wonderful." He looked to Jack. "But do you know the horse-trading business well enough?"

"*Ya*, I do. I am confident that I will be able to keep up with the demands of the community. And Grace here is a wealth of knowledge."

Grace bit back a smile to keep from showing her gratitude for his compliment.

"I see." Thomas lifted his chin as though to size Jack up. "Amos, where are you from?"

"Colorado."

Grace cleared her throat and lifted her eyebrows at him.

"Um…by way of New York. I moved from my Colorado community about eight years ago. We had many horses that came down from the mountains. When I was a bit younger, I trained as well as traded."

"I see," Thomas said again, and frowned. He glanced Leroy's way. "Leroy here has been prepared to…help the Millers. Isn't that correct, Grace?" Thomas looked for her to agree with what he wasn't saying.

That Leroy hoped to be her husband.

She placed two more plates on the table before finding the words to respond. "That is quite kind of Leroy, but we should have plenty of assistance from Amos and shouldn't need any extra help. But *denki*."

"No need to ever thank an Amish for aid," Thomas grumbled. "You should know that. It is what we do and what is expected." He stepped back to the door and held the handle. "I do wish I would have known you already had assistance coming. New York is a far distance to travel from. Especially when we already had someone ready to help here. Come along, Leroy."

Leroy's brown eyes widened and darkened in an instant from beneath his black hat, where his blond hair frizzed out over his ears. With his feet planted firmly, he said, loud and clear, "No." The reply didn't sound like a petulant child having a tantrum, but more like a threat.

"Is there a problem, Leroy?" Jack asked, his own eyes narrowing.

"You tell me," Leroy demanded. "Why haven't I ever heard of you before? Grace and I have courted. We held off after her *mamm*'s accident, but we hoped to be married eventually." He let that statement stand on its own.

Jack glanced Grace's way for a split second but didn't wait for her to respond. What could she say?

Leroy was right, and there was nothing she could do about it.

"She didn't want to impose," Jack answered, without missing a beat. He smiled and shook his head. "Imagine that. She worried that asking for help would cause strife. I told her she should have contacted me sooner. But it's just until Benjamin is able to return to the work he does so well. I'm sure it won't be long."

Thomas still frowned, but he nodded. "That would be good news, to have our Benjamin back to his old self."

Grace closed her eyes on a quiet prayer for it to be God's will. And not only for her sake. She knew the bishop would demand to know Benjamin's diagnosis soon. Oh, how she would love to say it wasn't dementia, after all.

The room grew heavy, with each of them having their silent doubts, but it was Leroy who broke the silence with an angry tone. "Something is going on around here, and I will find out what it is."

Grace came around the table to stand in front of him. She did her best not to hobble and give away the fact that her feet were burned. "I don't know what you're referencing. Can you explain?" she asked.

"I know about the trouble you've been having," Leroy said in a low tone, but didn't elaborate.

Suddenly, Jack was beside her. "What trouble? Is Grace not safe?"

Leroy shrugged. "Maybe. Maybe not." He leveled his gaze on her. "It will all depend on her choices, I suppose. In the end, it's all about our choices, isn't that right, Bishop?" Leroy asked over his shoulder to the man still holding the door.

"Yes, our choices have consequences. Sometimes we pay dearly."

A lump grew in Grace's throat. The threat was there for all to hear. She'd held Leroy off long enough. He was past antsy and would wait no more.

Grace had only one choice to make, no matter the consequence.

"I won't be marrying you, Leroy. You need to accept my decision as final."

Leroy stood quietly for a moment as his dark gaze flitted between Grace and Jack. "I see how it is."

"No, you don't," Jack said.

"Just where will you be sleeping? I will not have Grace's name tarnished."

"I am staying in the barn."

"With the horses?" Leroy asked quickly, then pressed his lips tight.

Grace felt Jack tense beside her. He'd noticed Leroy's quick response. A little too quick.

"I'll be fine, but yes, with the horses. Is that all right with you both?" Jack asked Leroy and the bishop.

Thomas nodded. "Of course. Hopefully, it won't be for long. *Komm*, Leroy. Now."

With the command from the elder, Leroy had no choice but to turn and leave. He gave one last warning glance at Grace before closing the door behind him. Nobody moved a muscle or said a word until the buggy creaked down the driveway and out of hearing distance.

"Has Leroy always been so tightly wound?" Jack asked.

Benjamin huffed from his chair. "My *frau* never cared for him. Go ask Amelia. She'll tell you Grace is too free for someone like him. He would strangle her with his severity."

Jack raised his eyebrows at Grace. "I think your *daed* speaks the truth."

"Except my *mamm* is dead, so no, he doesn't. You won't be asking her anything," Grace whispered, and went back to the table for her breakfast. Louder, she said, "Neither of you have to worry about me. I can handle Leroy, and I just did. There will be no more talk of marrying him."

Jack sat down. "You say that, but are you prepared for the consequence you may have just unleashed? You may think you can handle him, but that man knows something about the horses, and that could be dangerous."

Grace paused in spooning scrambled eggs onto her plate. "How do you mean, dangerous? Leroy's never hurt me."

"Because you've never given him reason to." Jack nodded to the door. "Until now."

Jack hitched up the two horses to the buggy and tied the thoroughbred to the rear. It felt wrong transporting the horse this way. He had a perfectly secure trailer attached to his truck, which was parked out of sight in the woods. But if he was going to pull off his latest undercover work, people couldn't suspect that he wasn't a real Amish man.

So the buggy would have to do.

He rubbed a hand down the neck of the sleek stallion. The horse widened his eyes and yanked on his tether. "It won't be a long walk," Jack assured him. "Before you know, you'll be back at home in your stall at the track." Jack gave him one last pat and walked around to climb up into the buggy.

Grace stepped from the house with a black satchel over her wrist. She still hobbled a bit in her boots. It would be a few days before her feet would be on the mend.

She stopped at the steps to the buggy and looked up at him. "Are you sure we should be bringing the horse back to Autumn Woods? Will it be safe for him there?"

"Only if you don't steal him again."

Grace sputtered. "But I didn't—"

Jack smiled at her shocked expression. "Don't forget I saw you with my own eyes," he said.

Her eyes narrowed up at him. "Are you fooling with me? Please tell me you are."

"Get in," he said. "It's going to take us a while to get there without my truck." Jack flicked the reins once Grace had situated herself in her seat beside him. The horses stepped out at a leisurely pace, and Jack thought it might take longer than he expected at this rate. "I think I owe the stallion an apology."

"Apology? To a horse?"

"*Ya*, I lied to him. I told him it wouldn't be long until we get there, but it's looking like we might not arrive until evening."

"Don't be ridiculous. It won't take much more than an hour. We'll be there by dinner."

"An hour? I thought these horses were good picks."

She shrugged, keeping her gaze straight ahead.

"They were. The Amish don't need the fast life. In fact, we slow our clocks down compared with the English."

"I remember," he admitted, but didn't hide his annoyance with the way of life he'd left behind. "I also remember how the Amish had their own set of rules to determine a person's innocence."

She glanced his way quickly. "If you mean the *ordnung*, yes, we have an established way of life to curb chaos among the community. It's needed if we are to continue in this fast-paced world of uncertainties."

Grace's eyes held some of that uncertainty in them. He could tell she was suddenly questioning being alone with him on the road. He thought it best to hold his tongue about his past and why he'd left his family. Or more like why his family had left him.

He cleared his throat and looked back at the road ahead. "So, you take the horses that fail the race test," he said, changing the subject back to their previous topic. He didn't need to hear how his family had been right in turning him away.

She let out a deep breath and faced forward again, too. "*Ya.* The owners at the track don't want them. They're happy to sell them to us and cut their losses."

Jack chewed on that bit of information as he drove the buggy over the hills. The road wound through the tall blue grasses of Kentucky horse country, but being early fall, the vibrant colors were changing into earthy golds. Snow would cover it all once winter set in.

Before them, the two horses paced in unison, their gaits perfectly matched. "They work well together," he said. "Did you purchase them, or did your *daed*?"

"I did." Grace fiddled with the strap of her black

satchel. When he glanced her way, he saw she wore a frown as she stared straight ahead. "He's been getting worse lately, but it's been a long time coming. It's only recently that I've been going to the track alone. I took him as long as I could, so people still thought he was the one doing the actual buying."

"But it's been you. For how long?" Jack asked, without looking her way. The methodic rotation of the wheels and the clip-clop of the horses encouraged a relaxed dialogue. Jack took the opportunity to dig a little deeper into Grace Miller's life. After all, she was still a suspect.

The profile of her small upturned nose lifted a bit. She frowned and said, "Before my *mamm* died."

"When was that?" he asked.

Grace sighed. "Nearly six months ago. Up until then she covered a lot for *Daed*, and I suppose I've tried to follow her lead, but…" Jack could feel tension and weariness exude from the woman beside him. She was in a hard place.

"I could tell by your visitors this morning that there are people waiting in the wings to take the reins from you. Why not let them, if all these responsibilities are taking their toll on you?"

Grace turned his way, her blue-green eyes watering up before him. "It's all I know."

"Horses, you mean?" Jack pulled the reins a bit to slow the buggy down. He gestured to the horse tied up behind them. "But you took a thoroughbred home and didn't know it."

"Don't remind me. You don't understand how tired I am. Keeping watch over *Daed* is constant. I've had to leave him often this last month, and while I am at the track, all I can do is worry for his safety home alone. I wasn't paying attention. I didn't check the tattoo IDs. I trusted that the ticket matched the horse, and I left for home as fast as I could."

Jack nodded. "*Ya*, watching you at the track, I did think you were in a hurry, but I figured that proved you were stealing, not rushing back to your ailing father at home. I'm sorry you have so much to deal with, and now you have an angered suitor, too."

Grace made a funny sound with her lips before rolling those pretty eyes upward. "He is not my suitor anymore. He hasn't been for a while."

"He didn't seem happy about those days ending. That concerns me. Especially since he seemed worried about me staying in the barn with the horses. Did you tell him that you had some horses taken from your barn?"

Grace shook her head. "Only Sheriff Maddox. I asked him to keep it a secret. I didn't want the community finding out. I feared…well, you know what I feared."

"A hostile takeover," Jack mumbled.

She huffed a laugh. "Something like that. But don't worry about Leroy. He really is harmless. If he wasn't, I would have learned that six months ago when I ended our courtship. I am certain sure he knows nothing about the horse thefts. At first, I had thought it was Leroy stealing them from the barn to make it look like I needed to hand over the job to a man, but now I know that wasn't the case."

Jack would withhold his opinion on Leroy's innocence until he learned more about the man. He also hoped Grace was innocent in all this, because he found the more time he spent with her, the more he liked her as a person. "You're different than any Amish woman I've ever met. It would have been nice if I had someone like you in my corner back home."

Grace waved his remark off. "All Amish women are hardworking."

"I wasn't talking about your work ethic."

"Then what?" Now Grace studied his profile as Jack realized he had said too much.

"Let's just say I had my own trouble in my community. It would have been nice to have someone fight beside me. Someone to believe in my innocence."

Grace's mouth fell open with shock. "You think I fight? You must know that is not a becoming trait for an Amish person, never mind a woman. It's unacceptable."

Jack shrugged. "That depends on who is benefiting from the fight." He looked her way and said, "And where your heart is when you decide to step in. Is it really bad to speak up for someone who might be innocent?"

Grace chewed on her lower lip for a moment, then asked, "Were you? Innocent, I mean?"

Jack couldn't answer her directly. He knew he'd played a part, even if he was innocent of the crime. "I was innocent where the law was concerned, but not in the eyes of my community. I let them down and no one would listen to why I felt I had to. They just assumed the worst."

"I'm sorry," Grace said. "I didn't mean to pry." She fiddled with her satchel strap again and faced forward.

Before Jack could drum up the gumption to come clean, a giggle erupted from beside him. He glanced her way to see her gawking at him with wide, laughing eyes.

"What?" he asked, and self-consciously rubbed his cheek. "Am I wearing my breakfast?"

"No, you're wearing my horse's hair." Her smile turned brilliant and the green of her eyes brightened. "I wondered how you made your hair grow to look Amish." Grace pointed to the horse on her side of the buggy. "You cut Peanut's tail!"

Jack stifled a laugh of his own at her wonderment. His response was simple. "Peanut and I were a perfect match."

Her pretty face blossomed pink in an endearing amusement that stirred something within Jack. Maybe it was the slow pace of the buggy or the rhythm of the horses' clip-clops that brought the past to him, but he doubted that was all. The reaction left him in an awkward silence, gazing straight ahead, as he tried to place the reason for the nostalgic feeling.

Was it a memory from his past?

Jack shook his head once, knowing the answer.

No. It was a longing. A desire for a place in his community, where sitting beside a pretty Amish woman who could be his companion in life was a perfectly good goal. But that was never to be. He was too different. He had a need to right wrongs. He didn't turn the other cheek, as was called for, but instead was a fighter. And as Grace said, that was not acceptable.

"Pull to the right," she told him nervously. "There's

a car coming up behind us driving too fast. Let them go around us."

Jack did as she asked, and also chastised himself for not noticing the situation first. He needed to keep his head out of the past and trained on the situation at hand.

The small white pickup truck zipped by in a roaring flash. As it raced by, Jack heard the rattle of its broken muffler and smelled the bad odor it emitted.

"He needs to get that fixed before the fumes kill him," Jack mumbled. "Do cars always get so close?" He looked Grace's way. Immediately, the driver's car problems and driving skills were the least of Jack's worries. Grace's complexion had faded to a pasty gray. He reached for her white-knuckled hands grasping the strap of her satchel. "What is it?"

She took a deep breath with her eyes closed before saying, "It was so loud. I feared it would spook the horses."

Jack assessed the animals in the front and back, and thought they'd handled the situation well. "Do they normally spook easily?"

She shook her head. "Not these horses, but we had one that did. Unfortunately, it was my mother driving the buggy the day a car scared the horse into a ditch and…" Grace swallowed and pressed her lips together. Her change in demeanor spoke for her.

Jack tightened his hand over hers. "Wait. Was your mother killed in a buggy accident?"

"The horse ran into a ditch and tipped the buggy onto her. She died in my arms when…I could finally get her out. I was thrown out the door before it rolled right over me. Nothing but a few scratches. But not her."

"The driver left you?"

Grace nodded, with tears in her eyes.

Anger flashed in Jack. He couldn't imagine such an injustice, but Grace's tears reminded him she didn't need his anger. How hard that must have been for her. "I didn't know. I thought she had been ill."

"No, she was stronger than any of us. She could have lived a lot longer. And I needed her to." Grace closed her eyes and nodded firmly. "Now I make sure the horses I buy at the track can withstand loud noises."

Jack didn't know why, but he felt there was much more to what really happened. A wrong had definitely been committed against Grace and her mother, and he couldn't let it go. After all, righting wrongs was what he did.

"It's been nearly six months." Grace frowned. "But it still doesn't feel real."

Jack wondered why he didn't know this information about Grace's *mamm*. "Did you report it?" he asked.

She shook her head. "I didn't want the media descending on us. Buggy accidents always bring them in, and with my *daed*... He wouldn't have been able to handle it, and I didn't want his illness to be known by everyone. Sheriff Maddox helped us keep her cause of death quiet—even with most of the community."

"The sheriff knew and didn't launch an investigation?" The idea irked Jack. Law enforcement officers weren't supposed to be passive. They were supposed to fight for justice.

"My *daed* had just bought the horse. I was thankful another Amish family hadn't acquired her yet. It was a bad purchase, and I vowed it wouldn't happen again."

Jack's red fury cleared and the truth came into focus. "You kept it a secret to protect your father."

Grace nodded. "It was a bad purchase," she repeated.

"Because if people learned your father wasn't able to do this job anymore, he would lose it. And so would you."

"Worse. *Daed* would have been ostracized." Grace's green eyes implored him to understand. Little did she know he knew the feeling on a personal level. "The sheriff helped me keep it a secret and said it was my mother's illness that caused her to go off the road. She was under the weather and couldn't focus. It wasn't a lie. She really wasn't feeling well that day."

"But Grace, that means you let someone go free who killed your mother."

She shrugged. "Cars and trucks are loud. It's not their fault if a horse gets spooked. The driver probably didn't even know what happened as he went past."

Jack struggled to understand Grace's reasoning. "You don't think your mother deserves justice?"

"I don't want to talk about it," she said, and turned to look at the passing scenery.

Silence ensued as Jack drove on, and eventually, the Autumn Woods Ranch and Racetrack came into view. He respected her request for ending the conversation, but said, "I'm trying to understand, but I need your honesty to do this. And to solve this case."

She swung her head to face him. "My *mamm*'s death has nothing to do with the horses, other than my *daed*'s poor purchase of one."

"Maybe, maybe not. I still need to know all the details if justice will be served."

Grace lifted her head haughtily. “That’s not a trait the Amish strive for, either. I forgave the person in the car that day, but I also vowed to do better here at the track, so that it never happens again.”

Jack scoffed as he pulled the reins, turning the horses into the long drive. “That’s another reason why I never made a good Amish man. For me, justice is all that matters.”

“If that’s what you think, then I will have to agree with you. You do not make a *gut* Amish man.”

SEVEN

The Autumn Woods stables were located at the back of a sprawling property beyond an oval racetrack and various small outbuildings. High up on a hill overlooking the property stood the two-story private home of the owner. The creamy-white house with high peaks and gleaming glass lent a prestigious glamour to the horse ranch. Jack whistled at the extravagant dwelling, then scanned the vast property. The track offered well-trained horses that were accustomed to pulling race carts and hearing loud noises. The owner had no reason to keep the slower horses, but the Amish welcomed such an animal, and so this was one instance the English and Amish worlds were allowed to intersect.

Grace instructed him to drive the buggy past the fenced-in track surrounded by tall spectator stands. They would go sit in them soon, when the practices began. For now, she pointed to the rear lot, where hitching posts stood along the side of the stable. No horses were tethered there, except for one still hitched to a racing cart. Grace looked around for a worker but found no one. Not a single person anywhere.

She tempered her annoyance, and said, "That's strange of them to leave the horse connected to its cart like that."

Jack pulled up alongside the animal and put the brakes on the buggy. Shaking his head, he said, "She's panting like she just raced and needs cooling down." He scanned the area. "Where is everybody? Is it always this quiet?"

"No, but I don't usually come on Sundays." Grace jumped from the buggy to assess the situation. Petting the animal's slick coat proved that Jack was right. She grew infuriated at such treatment. "Are they *ferhoodled*?" Grace quickly unhitched her. "She needs to be walked."

"You're going to do it?" Jack said, standing up in his seat.

"Do you see anyone else around? Of course I will walk her."

As she started to lead the horse toward the pasture, Jack called out, "Wait." He stepped down from the buggy.

She looked over her shoulder to see him reaching under his shirt for something. "What is that?" she asked in confusion, even as her mind registered what it was that he held in his hand. "You can't carry a gun," she whispered harshly. "The Amish don't carry guns."

"I'm not Amish anymore." He tucked the weapon in his palm and held it close as he stepped up beside her, still looking around warily.

"But you're pretending to be. People will know in an instant you're not."

"It gives me extra strength and protection."

She scoffed, her lips pursed. “You’ll never know how strong you are as long as you rely on a weapon.”

“I’m not about to find out. Now walk,” he told her. “Something doesn’t feel right. I know it’s not a race day, but it’s too quiet. I feel like someone was expecting us and took flight. Or went to a hiding place.” He shook his head. “I don’t like being caught off guard.”

The horse nickered as Grace led her around, patting her gently. “I don’t feel good about this,” she said nervously.

“Me neither. There are too many trees and buildings someone could be hiding behind.”

“I was talking about the gun.”

He scoffed. “You’ll change your mind if someone starts shooting at us.” He pointed toward the back of the stables. “Stay to the right. We can use the building as cover if need be.”

“I disagree,” she said stubbornly. “There must be a better way.”

“Like a pitchfork?”

Grace glanced at Jack. He was daring her to deny it, his eyebrows raised. “I didn’t intend to use the farm tool as a weapon,” she said in her defense.

“Well, even though it was pointed at me, I’m glad you had it. It showed me you value your life. Which is why I need you to see the necessity of me having a weapon. I’m a lawman now, and this is part of my life. It protects me and it protects you. After last night’s shootout, it’s a must-have. I would hate to be caught empty-handed and have you pay for it with your life. Don’t ask me to not do my job to my fullest capacity. It would be too dangerous for us both.”

She frowned but nodded. "I'm supposed to value God's peaceful ways, but you're right. I do also value my life. It's an argument I have with *Daed* all the time." As they walked the horse out behind the long building, she took in the beauty of the Kentucky landscape around them, but a bit of growing guilt tainted the serene scenery. She decided to come clean with him. "To let you in on a little secret, I actually wished I had brought my *daed*'s hunting rifle out to the barn."

"Now *that's* a sight I would have liked to have seen. Although the pitchfork was inspiring." He smirked, but as they turned at the corner of the stable, his smile fell from his lips. He pointed his free hand toward something ahead of them. "Do you know why that white truck is parked here?"

Grace shrugged. "It's always parked there. It belongs to one of the stable hands."

"It's the same truck that gunned its engine as it passed us earlier. I think we found the person who alerted people to our visit."

Grace couldn't be sure one way or the other. When the truck had whizzed past, her eyes had been closed, while she prayed for the sound not to spook the horses. "It may have been a white truck, but this is horse country. Nearly every English person has a truck, many of them white."

"True," Jack conceded. "Only time will tell when the owner starts the engine. You can be certain sure I'll be listening for it." He sniffed deeply as they walked closer to it. "I don't smell the offensive odor the muffler gave off, but that doesn't mean anything."

"Even if it is the same truck, it still doesn't mean

anything. I think you're overreacting. Let's take this horse inside, and I'll introduce you to the stable hands. They're all very nice and respectful."

"I'm sure they are, but don't forget someone passed a thoroughbred to you in place of the standardbred you bid on. At least one of them is corrupt."

As much as Grace didn't want to believe it, she had to agree with him. Once could have been a mistake, but more than that was deliberate. Yet who could it be?

"Steven is a fair man," she said, thinking of each of the hands that she and her father had dealt with over the years. "He's the oldest of them all. His nephew Liam is the youngest, around twenty. Kind of quiet, but he's good with the horses. I can't see either of them stealing animals, never mind using me to do it."

"How many people work in the stables?"

Grace mentally counted the people she'd seen in the past. "I can't be sure, but when I come to pick up the horses, it's usually Steven or Liam who brings me the ones I bid on."

"Has there ever been anyone else, maybe someone you'd never seen before?"

"I don't recall…though maybe there was one time." She bit her lower lip and frowned. "I'll admit that in the past few months I've been in a hurry to return home. I might have turned over the claim number and not looked closely at the person I handed it to. Or, apparently, the horse I bought."

"Don't beat yourself up over it. Whoever is behind this probably saw your situation and used it to their advantage. Had anyone mentioned the thefts to you when you came the last few times?"

"Not at all. It was business as usual."

Jack searched the area as he seemed to be considering her words. "So, they kept the thefts under wraps. Someone alerted the FBI, but didn't share the knowledge with the staff or public. That tells me the whistleblower thinks it's an in-house job."

A car's motor broke the silence and interrupted their thoughts. Grace glanced up and saw a black sports car racing down the hill from the big mansion above. It curved around a bend in the driveway and drove past them at a fast clip. Suddenly, the driver hit the brakes and screeched to a halt. Gravel spit out from the tires as the car abruptly reversed, coming back to them.

The tinted window of the passenger side lowered until the driver became visible. He removed a pair of dark sunglasses and eyed them quizzically. Anger contorted his face and piercing dark eyes. "What are you two doing back here, and with my horse?"

Grace trembled at the blatant hostility in the man's voice. Never had she experienced such distaste coming at her. But worse, she felt her own anger rolling deep within her. Before she could control her wrath, she shouted back at the man, "How dare you treat your horse this way? You don't deserve her."

Instantly, Grace wanted to swallow the words back, especially when she felt Jack tense beside her and get ready to use his weapon. The idea of him shooting because she'd lost control of her tongue turned her anger into nausea.

The man stepped from his car and slammed the door. He stomped around the hood and came at them, pointing his finger. His frame exuded strength and even though he was in his late fifties, the man could deliver on his threat. His blond hair fell in his face and covered one eye. His rageful look told her she'd gone too far.

A soft answer turns away wrath.

The Scripture always rested at the forefront of Grace's mind. Not that it did any good to her a moment ago. But it gave her the power to speak quickly and kindly now, hoping she could steer the situation to a peaceful outcome.

"I want an answer. What are you doing with my horse?" he yelled.

Grace spoke in a quiet voice. "She was left hitched to the cart. She had just been raced. We found her alone and were walking her to cool her off."

The man pushed his mussed hair from his face. His lips snarled, but his next scathing look wasn't directed at her. This time it was aimed at the barn, along with his curled fists. "I can't trust anyone in there to do their job. I should fire them all." He reached for the horse's bridle. "I'll take her from here. Sorry, but I've lost too many horses already. And Game Changer is priceless."

Grace glanced up at Jack. His pensive expression told her he was considering his opinion of the man. As she was about to speak, he shook his head once to stop her.

"How have you lost your horses?" Jack asked.

"Thieves. I've lost three males in four months." His anger reddened his face, and he yanked on the horse's bridle to pull her forward.

"Please, go easy," Grace said without a thought. "I mean, please, don't take it out on her."

The man stopped and studied Grace with speculative eyes. He slowly turned to Jack and gave him his full attention. With his anger tempered, he gave Jack a single nod. "I'm sorry. Things have been upsetting around here. I've had to call the police to investigate, but no one has found any leads. I don't want to lose any more horses, but I feel like I'm doing this all alone. My father passed away a year ago. He was the brains behind the ranch. Really understood horses. I wish I'd paid more attention. Now all I can do is trust my workers to know what to do." He waved his hand as he pulled the horse with him, calling over his shoulder, "I don't know why I'm telling you this. Maybe it's because you're Amish. I really hope I can trust you, or all is definitely lost."

"What's your name?" Jack asked him.

With his hand on the door to the stables, he said, "Edmund Barone."

"You're the owner of Autumn Woods?"

Edmund glanced at Grace. His gaze locked on hers in a way that made her feel as though he expected her to answer. She didn't know him, and honestly never remembered seeing him around the track or stable. "I remember your father," she responded with a shrug.

"But not me, I know. I'm a prodigal son who returned home too late," Edmund looked to Jack and answered his question. "I'm in charge around here now, yes."

"I'm Jack Kaufman. And this is Grace Miller. Her father is the Amish horse trader who's been coming here for years." Jack dropped his hands to his sides in a nonchalant way. Grace was glad to see the gun was back in its hiding place but knew he could have it at the ready in an instant if need be.

Edmund Barone took a moment to register what

Jack had just told him. He quickly relaxed with a smile. "I've heard about your father. Nice man, from what I was told. Haven't seen him since I left town years ago, but I see your resemblance to your parents." He cleared his throat and said, "Well, at least your dad." Edmund then looked back at Jack and asked, "Are you taking over for him?"

Grace tried to hide a frown. Even the English didn't believe this was a job for a woman. She lifted her chin and said boldly, "Actually, I am."

Surprise washed over Edmund's face. Then he slowly smiled and rubbed his chin. "Perfect," he said. "I look forward to seeing you around here more. I think you'll fit right in."

Grace nodded but wasn't sure what he meant by his comment. It didn't feel like a compliment. It felt almost sinister. Here she was, bringing back his horse, but now wondered if she should have handed over the animal. She noticed Jack's hesitancy, as well, and knew he was concerned.

"What now?" she asked when Edmund had disappeared inside the stables.

Jack glanced up at the big house on the hill. "I'd like to learn a little more about him. It wouldn't be the first time an owner perpetrated a crime for the insurance money. And those horses are worth a pretty penny."

"I never thought of that. The Amish don't take out insurance policies. I always thought it was to keep us relying on God and our community, but perhaps our ways are also to preserve honesty. Money can cause evil intentions."

"They don't call it the root of all evil for nothing,"

Jack said. "Come on, I want to get the stolen thoroughbred back to your house before anyone realizes he's here. I'm not leaving him till I can figure out if the owner is involved."

"He said he's contacted the police. We can ask Sheriff Maddox to confirm that."

Jack scoffed at the idea as Grace fell into step with him. They circled back around the stable to where her buggy and horses were still hitched to the post.

But they weren't alone.

Liam Byler stood near the back of the buggy, feeding the stolen horse an apple with one hand and petting him with the other.

"*Hallo*, Liam," Grace said as they neared.

The young man abruptly turned and moved back. He rubbed his hands down his blue work pants a few times. "Hello. I'm sorry," he said in a hushed voice. "I didn't mean to— I mean, I was only giving him a treat. I hope that's okay."

"Of course," Grace assured him. He rarely spoke to her, and this was the most he probably had ever said to her at one time. "I'm sure he's happy about that. You wouldn't happen to have two more for my other horses, would you?"

Liam jammed his hands into his side pockets and pulled out two more apples, as well as a piece of paper. The small slip fluttered in the breeze before it drifted to the ground. With his hands full, Grace bent to retrieve the paper. It was a claim ticket just like the ones she turned in when picking up a horse.

Liam handed Jack the apples and quickly snatched the ticket from Grace. "I can't lose that. My uncle would kill me." He stepped back. "I have to go." And with that he pivoted, hurried to the gate into the track and slipped inside.

Jack fed the two horses their apples as he watched Liam go. "Is he always so nervous?"

"He doesn't talk much, so I'm not sure. I just go into the stable and hand him or his *onkel* Steven my ticket, and they bring me the horse."

Jack scanned the track area. "It doesn't look like much is going on today. We'll have to return another day. Let's get this horse back. Then we'll make our plans for our next move."

"Won't keeping the horse invite more danger to my home?"

"We won't be. My supervisor will know where he can go for safekeeping until I learn more about the people who work here and their boss." Jack stood by the buggy's door, behind Grace.

She slowly climbed into it. Glancing around the ranch, she questioned her safety here for the first time ever. "I don't want to believe anyone here could mean me harm."

Jack climbed up and settled back into the driver's seat. "Well, believe it. And don't forget, they set you up to pay for a crime." He flicked the reins, and the horses set out at a leisurely pace once again. "Unless you have something to share with me. Care to come clean?" He raised his eyebrows in question.

"You mean if I am the real thief, after all?"

"Or if you know why someone would want you to pay for the crime. And why they would shoot at you."

"I have no idea." Grace shook her head. "It's absurd."

"Think on it, because no matter how absurd you believe it is, they'll be back to finish the crime. And if you're not ready, you will fall right into their trap."

It was an hour later when Jack drove the buggy back into Grace's driveway and up to the barn doors. Locking the brake, he said, "I'll put up the horses. Nic will be here shortly to take the thoroughbred into custody."

"I can help with the horses, but I need to check on *Daed* first. I'll be right back." Grace stepped down from the buggy and walked around the rear. As she passed the stolen horse, she stopped to pat his cheek and peer into his glassy eyes. "It won't be long before you are safe."

He huffed in return. She patted him once more and went to the house and her father.

She had left Benjamin at the table with a task of shucking sweet corn ears from the fall season. She'd left him with two bushels, about a hundred cobs, but knowing her father, she was sure he'd be meticulous about removing every piece of silk. She expected to find most of the corn still left for her to husk. She had so many fruits and vegetables to can for the winter, and as her father became more and more distant and distracted, she accepted the workload before her.

Grace unlocked the kitchen door and opened it wide. Bright yellow ears of sweet corn were stacked on the table in a neat heap, each placed with precision into a pyramid shape. Grace smiled at her *daed*'s work ethic.

He might be losing his memory, but his identity as a hard worker was part of him.

"Daed?" she called out. "We're home!"

Grace walked into the living room and stood at the bottom of the stairs. She listened for sounds of her father up in his room, but no response came.

She took the steps slowly at first, then sped up when he didn't emerge from his opened door at the top. She walked to his room but found it empty.

Grace searched the other two bedrooms, with no success. Pausing at the window in her room that overlooked the rear yard and garden, she hoped to find him working in it.

There was no sign of him anywhere.

"Daed!" Grace raced back out into the hall and down the stairs with thudding feet. Ignoring the pain in her feet, she called, "*Daed!* Where are you?"

She ran through the living room to the kitchen, praying she would find him there now. Maybe she had walked right by him when she'd entered through the back door. Her hope was silly, but she held on to it with all she had in her. The alternative was too much to bear. The idea that her father was missing scared Grace more than horse thieves.

"Daed!" she yelled, as she opened the rear door and stepped out onto the porch. She gripped the railing with white-knuckled hands as her heart rate picked up. She called out again, but knew it was no use. She ran down the steps, scanning the pastures, fields and woods, all the way over to the ridge.

"Grace?" Jack stepped from the barn. He picked up

his pace until he stood before her, his hands reaching for her upper arms. “What’s wrong?” he demanded.

She felt him give her a shake, but his face blurred before her. *“Daed!”* she gasped, still hoping her father would appear from the cornfield or from behind the barn. Hot tears streamed down her cheeks, but she couldn’t stop them even if she tried. Fear overtook her. “He’s gone,” she cried out. “*Daed* is gone!”

EIGHT

Alarm tightened Jack's chest and hit his stomach like a sucker punch. He held a frantic Grace at arm's length and fought the urge to pull her in close, to give her comfort and wipe away her tears. Her visible fear provoked him to want to fix whatever it was that caused her such distress. All he knew in this moment was that Grace needed him.

Then her words sank in and the meaning of them explained her state.

Benjamin Miller was missing.

"Did you check the whole house?" he asked, as he let her go and went to see for himself. His heavy boots on the wood floors echoed back at him as he searched the house. But there was no sign of Benjamin anywhere, not in the house, or the barn, or the trees beyond. Everywhere Jack looked, he returned with no success.

And no comfort for Grace.

When Jack came back from the woods, he found her hitching the buggy back up.

"Where are you going?" he asked.

"To Sheriff Maddox. I need help searching. It will

be dark soon. I have to find him." Grace ran around the barn at a frantic pace, readying the horses.

"What makes you think he wandered off? How do you know he wasn't taken?"

"Taken?" Grace froze at the closest stall. "Who would take an old Amish man?"

Jack shrugged. "Maybe someone trying to get to you? Maybe our horse thief returned for the thoroughbred and found him gone, so took your father instead." Jack looked around the barn for any clues of a ransom note. Everything was in its place and as they had left it that morning. "I need to search the house again."

She opened the door to lead the horse out. "He's not in there. We've already looked."

"Now I'm looking for any signs of a kidnapper."

"Well, while you do that, I'm getting the sheriff."

Jack stepped in her way. "I'm sorry, Grace, but I can't let you leave. It's too dangerous. I'll get my phone and call Sheriff Maddox for you."

"You're not supposed to have a phone, remember? You're pretending to be Amish. He'll know you aren't."

She was right, but if he had to break his cover with anyone, he was fine with it being the local law enforcement. "If your *daed* was taken, then I consider it to be worth it."

"But what if he wasn't? What if he just walked off? He's so confused lately, I'm sure that's it."

"Either way, he could be in danger, and we don't have time to ride out for the sheriff."

She chewed on her lower lip for a moment. "Can we just check one place before you call?"

Every second ticking by was one second too much.

But Jack sighed and asked, "Why do you think Benjamin wandered off? Has he done this before?" Jack took her elbow to lead her out of the barn.

Grace squeezed her eyes shut and her lips trembled. "Once. A couple months ago I found him where *Mamm* died."

Jack felt the kick of pain he witnessed on Grace's face. He fisted his hands to keep from reaching for her. "You're trying to keep so much going. I'm surprised you're still standing." He placed an arm over her shoulders and fought the urge to pull her close. The desire was strong, but he pushed it away. "Come on, we'll start there. Can you think of any other place he might go? Maybe somewhere he went with your *mamm,* as well?"

Grace stopped and glanced up, a look of realization washing over her face. "The ridge." She pointed to the cliff that abutted the property. "There's a dirt road up to it. They used to walk there to watch the sunset together."

"Sounds pleasant. Can we drive it?"

She hesitated. "It's pretty steep. I wouldn't want to put the horses through that."

"I was talking about my truck."

Grace pressed her lips tight but made the right choice. She headed toward the trees. "*Ya*, but if he's not there, we have to get Sheriff Maddox."

"That's fine, but if he's not there, we have to consider criminal behavior. You have something the thieves want."

Stark fear settled on her face, blanching it. "Would they take an old man with dementia?"

"Without blinking."

"Oh, Jack." Grace reached up to pull on the strings of her *kapp*. Her chin trembled.

It was the first time she had used his first name. Up until now, she'd kept the formality of his title, automatically determining their relationship. It had set a boundary that now had been breached, and Jack wasn't sure how he felt about that.

And yet he wanted to hear it again.

Part of him liked the sound of his name on her lips, but another part reminded him that he'd never make a *gut* Amish man—and also that he'd come here to arrest her.

"What about the thoroughbred?" she asked. "What if they took *Daed* so we would leave the horse behind while we searched? Can we take him with us so he's safe?"

"The idea did cross my mind." Jack studied her eyes, more green in the afternoon sunlight. And clearly concerned. "You really don't want them taking the thoroughbred, do you?"

She jerked at his question and looked at him in confusion. "Of course not. Why—why would you think so?" Then her eyes darkened and her lips pursed. "I see. You still think I'm involved in this. What can I possibly say to make you believe me?"

Jack frowned. "I may regret this, but I think you just said it."

"I did? What did I say?"

Jack's frown faded as he reached for her wrist. "Come on. We'll get the truck and load up the horse. Our first priority is finding Benjamin."

With no argument there, the two of them moved his

truck from its hiding place and settled the thoroughbred in the trailer. As they pulled out of the driveway, Jack checked his phone messages to see if Nic had called him back. The sooner the horse was picked up, the sooner Jack could start investigating deeper.

He glanced to the passenger seat at Grace. True concern tensed every one of her muscles. Her hands fisted in her lap showed her anxiety. And yet she faced the danger with courage.

Jack faced forward, knowing that even if he unloaded the horse, he would still have to keep Grace with him. In fact, he needed her to lure these criminals out. She was the unsuspecting target, the perfect person to use for their gains.

But what were those gains, exactly? And who was benefiting?

"*Daed*'s not here this time. This is where she died," Grace said quietly, cutting into his unanswered questions. She pointed toward the side of the road, and he slowed to a stop.

"Your *mamm*?"

She nodded, a deep, aching sadness on her face.

The sight would cripple him if he didn't focus on his reason for being here. He looked away, fixing his attention on the surrounding area. "You were right. You didn't get far from home." Jack took notice of the marshy lands at the side of the road, where water collected, filling the ditch after rains. "That was a steep fall."

Grace nodded. "If we were just a few feet farther up the road, we would have been fine, but the wheels sank immediately and tipped us over."

Jack looked up and down the road. "It's so isolated out here. Do many cars drive by here?"

"Not a lot, but they do come out from town from time to time."

Jack wanted to get out and walk around, but now was not the time. They needed to find Benjamin. He put his truck back into gear and drove toward the dirt road coming up on the left. "I assume this is the way up to the ridge?"

Grace nodded and pointed. Words escaped them both as the moment of clarity neared. In just a few minutes they would know if Benjamin had wandered off.

Or if he had been taken.

As the truck ascended up the hill, it scraped past hanging branches, and the two of them sat in a heavy silence. Grace leaned forward, her attention jumping in all directions as they entered the clearing. Her lips moved in what appeared to be a silent prayer.

"I don't see him," she said in a worried voice when they reached the top, her hand already on the door latch.

"Hold on. Let me drive closer to the edge." The last word slipped out before he realized how it would affect her.

"The edge?" She covered her mouth to stifle a wail. "I didn't even think about him going over—"

"And don't," Jack said, cutting her off abruptly. "I shouldn't have said that. I'm sorry." He pulled the truck up as far as he could and parked it. For a moment, neither of them moved. "Would you like me to search the area?"

It was the easiest way he could ask the question. The

idea of her seeing her father at the bottom of the ridge had him wishing she would say yes.

"No. I will look." Grace opened the door with sudden determination and jumped from the truck.

Jack quickly opened his own side. He should have known she wouldn't back down from this. She'd proved time and time again that she was a fighter—whether she wanted to accept that about herself or not.

She stood at the edge with her back to him, looking down but not saying a thing.

"Grace?" Jack stepped up behind her and carefully put a hand on her small shoulder. He expected her to flinch, but instead she leaned against him with a heart-wrenching wail.

Jack took a breath and dared to look.

Grace buried her face in the crook of Jack's neck. The collar of his crisp white shirt absorbed her tears of fear as the inconceivable took root. She trembled at the idea of her *daed* facing such an act of terror. Even before his mind deteriorated from the dementia, he had been a soft-spoken, gentle man.

Grace lifted her hands to Jack's chest and grabbed hold of his black suspenders as if they could hold her up like a lifeline. But even with his strong frame beside her and his arms moving to envelop her, Grace couldn't keep her legs from weakening.

"They've got him, Jack. He's not here. They've taken him, haven't they?" She spoke into his neck and felt him swallow hard against her cheek. "*Daed* has been kidnapped by these thieves. We have to find him. Oh, please, *Gött*, please help us find him."

Jack rubbed her back gently. "Now, we don't know that for sure. We'll call the sheriff and start a search party. We could still find him out here."

Grace lifted her face in time to see Jack's doubtful expression. He quickly glanced away, taking his thoughts with him. But his jaw tightened and his eyes, when he looked back at her again, were dark, the ebony shade she recognized from the night she'd first met him in the barn.

The night he'd tracked her down and held a gun on her.

"Can you find him?" she asked. "Can you track my father?"

Jack locked his gaze on hers. With their faces so close, Grace could feel his breath brushing against her cheek. She'd never been this close to any man other than her father. She knew she should back away and step out of his arms, but his presence was the only thing keeping her on her feet.

Except now her knees trembled for other reasons than fear.

Grace recognized the strange feeling filling her belly with inappropriate reactions. She couldn't look to this man for anything but assistance. Yet there was a power about him that confused the order of her life and what she thought she desired.

Grace flattened her palms against him and used her declining strength to push back and out of such an immoral proximity with Jack Kaufman.

An English man.

An English man who would bring chaos to her life.

His arm hovered between them with his hand outstretched to her. Slowly, his long fingers curled into a fist, and he dropped it to his side.

"I will do whatever I have to to find him. I promise, Grace. You can count on me."

"Can I?" She lifted her chin and faced him eye to eye. "Because when I look at you, all I see is a man who is *gut* at pretending. I also see someone who doesn't trust in his own strength—or *Gött*'s, for protection and guidance. How do you know you can find *Daed* when you left *Gött* behind?"

Jack's jaw tightened at her words. He lowered his eyes and turned to face the drop-off over the ridge. "I never said I left *Gött* behind. I said my family left me."

"They must have had a *gut* reason," Grace said, but Jack seemed to not be listening to her suddenly. She stopped talking and watched him study the land below.

Her house could be partially seen through the trees, a tiny miniature at this distance. The back of the barn, as well, but everything else was blocked by the woods.

"What do you see?" she asked.

He squinted, then moved away from her without responding and walked closer to the edge. The rim dipped a bit there, and he bent and crouched down. When he stood, he had a beer can in his hand, wrapped in a handkerchief.

"Do people usually come up here to party?" he asked.

Grace gave his question a thought, then shook her head. "Not that I know of. I've never seen such a thing. It's private land."

"I'm assuming this isn't your father's can."

"Absolutely not." Grace bit her lip. She hoped not, anyway. "He wouldn't have before—"

"And he wouldn't still," Jack interrupted. "I wasn't being serious." He held up the can and studied it. "This was dropped here recently. Judging by the view of your home, this has been a lookout for our thieves."

Grace shuddered. "You mean they've been watching us?"

Jack nodded. "Let's get back and call the local law enforcement. I'd like to have them comb the area for any other clues these guys left behind. I'll have the prints run on this can."

"But first, they need to find my *daed*." Grace allowed him to usher her back to the truck. She wrapped an arm around her stomach, scrunching her apron in her hand.

"Our first priority." He opened the door for her and held it while she climbed into the cab. Before he shut it, he said, "If he was taken, we'll find out soon enough."

"How do you know?"

Jack nodded to the horse trailer behind the truck. "We have what they want. They'll need to arrange for the ransom."

"I hope it's soon." Grace frowned. "He must be so scared."

Jack's eyelids closed for a brief moment. When he opened them, he slammed the door and stomped around the front of the pickup. Once in, neither of them said another word as they returned to the house.

Jack drove to the back of the property and pulled into his truck's hiding place. He killed the engine, leaving them both in silence.

"I need to make the phone call," he told her.

"How will you explain having a phone?" Grace asked.

"I'll just say I bought it for the trip here, for safety. I can say my bishop gave me his consent."

Grace knew it was the fastest way to find her father, but she couldn't give her approval to a lie. She opened the truck door. Without looking back, she said, "Do what you think is best."

She left Jack there and made her way out of the woods and to the barn. As she passed the building, the sound of crunching gravel drew her attention to the road.

A green sheriff's cruiser pulled down her driveway and stopped in front of her house. Grace froze on the spot, unsure what she should do.

She looked back and saw Jack by his truck, making the call. Without a thought, she ran back to him.

"Stop!" she yelled. "Sheriff Maddox is here."

"Now?" Jack asked, with the phone to his ear.

She nodded, and he pushed a button on the device. In the next second, it was gone from view, hidden like his gun. Jack was around the truck in a flash and by her side.

Together, they rushed to the house, having no more time to waste to find her father. But when they came within sight of the sheriff's car, Jack stopped in his tracks, pulling Grace to a halt with his hand in hers.

"On the porch," he said, directing her attention there.

The next second, Grace let go of Jack's hand and took off in a run. *"Daed!"* she yelled. *"Du bischt haim!"* Her father was home. She ran at breakneck speed toward Benjamin, who stood beside Sheriff Maddox on the porch. When she reached him, she threw her arms around him and cried out in relief. He was really home. And safe.

Grace cupped her father's cheek as Jack approached the bottom of the steps. She smiled down at him, but her smile slipped away when she saw his serious expression directed at Sheriff Maddox.

Jack's arms folded over his chest. He looked at Hank and said, "Why do you have Benjamin? Do you have any idea the pain you have caused Grace by taking him from his home?"

Sheriff Maddox looked to Grace and back at Jack before replying. He tilted his head with a smirk and said, "I'll explain right after you come clean with the Millers on why you left your Colorado community in the first place. Because it sure wasn't to come help them, like you said. More like to help yourself to what isn't yours. Isn't that correct, Mr. Kaufman?"

NINE

"You leave my *brudder* alone," Benjamin said to Sheriff Maddox. "We don't take kindly to law enforcers butting into our business. Amos hasn't done anything wrong. You tell him, Amos. Tell him you haven't done anything wrong."

"Amos?" Sheriff Maddox squinted. "I assure you Benjamin that this is not your brother. He's a con artist and your thief."

Jack locked his gaze on Hank Maddox's and made sure the sheriff knew he wasn't playing his game. "Yes, Benjamin is confusing me for his brother, but whatever *you* think you know about me is also wrong."

"So, you aren't Jack Kaufman of the San Luis Valley? The one who had a run-in with the law?" Hank's eyebrows raised, and he dared Jack to deny the accusation.

Grace inhaled sharply and quickly turned to push her father into the house. "*Komm, Daed.* I need you to finish the corn, so I can ready it for canning."

"We have so much work to do before winter," Benjamin said, and let her usher him in. "Amos, don't pay any mind to the officer. He doesn't understand our ways."

Grace moved her father inside before he could say anything else. Then she shut the door and faced the two lawmen.

"Sheriff, you know not to take my father's words as always clear and accurate. He gets confused."

"Hank," the sheriff reminded her again.

Grace sighed with a slight frown. "You have done so much for us, especially with keeping *Mamm*'s death out of the news. He wouldn't have been able to handle the attention. I am grateful to you for that, but I must ask you never to take my father out of here without my knowing it. I feared the worst when we came home and found him gone."

Hank shook his head. "I'm sorry you were scared, but I didn't take him. I found him wandering around in town by the library. You really shouldn't be leaving him here alone. It's not safe, Grace."

She looked to Jack.

Before Sheriff Maddox made her feel any worse than she already did, Jack spoke up for her. "Grace knows her father better than anyone. She knows what he can handle. How about you let her decide what's best for him?"

"Fine by me," Hank responded. "I think that's a great idea. Would you like to tell her the truth of where you come from, or shall I? I think I know their needs better than a man with a record."

Jack had a decision to make on whether he would come clean with her about his past. If he didn't, there was no telling what else Hank would say. Or make up.

"You are mistaken," Jack informed the sheriff. "I was never convicted of any wrongdoing."

"In the eyes of your community you were." Hank turned his back on Jack and faced Grace. "Can we talk privately? I have a lot you need to know."

She folded her arms in a protective gesture, her fingers gripping the sleeves of her light blue dress.

Jack fought the urge to reach for her. She looked unsure of everything right now. He was certain all she wanted to do was go inside and be with her father after such a traumatic day. When her questioning gaze fell on him, Jack took a step up the stairs to be closer to her. "You do what you have to, but I would appreciate a chance to defend myself," he said.

Grace shook her head. "Stay." To Hank, she said, "Anything you need to tell me, you can say in front of Jack."

"I really don't think that's wise," the sheriff replied. "You need to trust me. I know what's best for y—"

"Wrong," she said, cutting him off. "*I* know what's best for me."

Jack bit back a smile, and felt his chest swell in appreciation of Grace's strong nature.

Hank cleared his throat and nodded once. "I understand. Have it your way, but don't say I didn't warn you." His expression darkened. "This man was accused of trafficking guns across state lines."

Grace shot Jack a surprised look. But it was her ensuing frown that cut him to the quick. She believed the worst of him. But could he fault her? He'd come into her life to arrest her. He carried a gun even though she'd voiced her disdain. She didn't know him enough to listen to his side. His own family had known him their whole lives, and none of them had defended him. How could he expect anything more from Grace?

"It was one gun," Jack said in his own defense. "Not that the number of weapons matters. It was still a crime. However, the charges were dropped, and I was able to go free. There's more to the story, if you're interested in hearing it."

"I'm not," Hank said. "All I'm interested in is protecting this unsuspecting family from someone who means them harm."

"That's not me," Jack said. He considered blowing his cover and coming clean with the lawman. He supposed eventually he would have to, when arrests were made, but until there were better leads to the criminals, Jack needed to keep his profession secret. "I care about this family and am here to help."

"I've been told your family ousted you from the community eight years ago. Whether charges were dropped or not. So where have you been all this time?"

Jack held back from sharing about his time in the police academy, followed by his employment with the government. He'd been given a second chance, and guarded his law enforcement cases very seriously. "After I left home, I found a new community to be a part of. People who believed in me and shared my desire for justice to be served. I want to offer that to Benjamin and Grace. It's why I came when I heard about the stolen horses."

"Convenient, I'd say." Sheriff Maddox pursed his lips in speculation. "And a little too heroic. How do I know you didn't come to steal them yourself?"

"I'm here all the time. Right, Grace?" Jack asked the conflicted young woman. Her eyes were closed, and he knew he couldn't count on her to back him, even though it wasn't a lie. "Well, it doesn't matter. It's the tru—"

"Ya." She cut in, her shoulders pushed back now and her head held high. "Jack hasn't left here since the night he arrived. Woke me up from a sound sleep when I was supposed to be guarding the horses. If he came to take them, he could have done so right away. Instead, he's helping me figure out who *is* stealing them."

"Helping you find the thief?" Hank scoffed. "He's an all-around helpful guy. But isn't that like the fox guarding the henhouse?" He eyed Jack as if to sum him up.

"Jack is not a thief, Sheriff. I can promise you that," Grace said firmly.

He turned to stare at her. "If you say so, Grace. But don't say you haven't been warned. Whether he's a criminal or not, you are housing someone with questionable decision-making skills."

"I'll take your warning to heart," Grace said. "Now if you'll excuse us, we really need to attend to *Daed*."

Hank moved to the stairs. "I'll be on my way, but from now on, keep a closer watch on your father. He's getting worse, Grace, and I won't be able to hide your secret much longer. Bishop Bontrager is growing more and more concerned."

Grace's face blanched instantly. Jack watched her swallow hard as panic set in. "The bishop has come to you? He would never unless—"

"Not the bishop directly, but someone in the community did."

"Who?"

Hank frowned. "Now, Grace, don't put me in the middle. I've honored your request to keep your *Mamm*'s cause of death and Benjamin's illness private. Allow me to do the same for others."

Grace sighed, then nodded. "Of course, Sheriff. Forgive me. I only ask because I do believe whoever stole the horses may be someone in the community wanting to take my father's position."

"I see. And that may be the case, so if I think you may be correct, I'll break the confidence, all right?"

Grace gave the sheriff a slight smile. "I appreciate that, *denki*."

Sheriff Maddox tipped his hat to Grace, but ignored Jack completely as he trounced down the stairs. He made his way to his cruiser and drove off.

Even after his car disappeared from view, Grace remained silent. Jack stood in a state of expectancy, waiting for her to determine his place in her life. The last time he'd done so, it was to await the decision of the elders after his Amish hearing. The bishop had responded with his walking papers. Would Grace respond the same?

"If you would rather I continue my investigation from afar, I would understand," he said.

Grace's eyelashes fluttered as she shook her head. "Don't be silly. I'm sure whatever happened in your community has a perfectly valid explanation, or you wouldn't be an FBI agent today."

Jack shrugged. "True enough." Even though he'd rather forget what had happened eight years ago, he wasted no time in telling her. "I helped an English girl escape an abusive relationship one night. She had me grab her father's gun before we left. She took it with her, but my fingerprints were on the weapon. Unfortunately for her and for me, she went back to the boyfriend. He took the gun and used it to rob a convenience store. With my prints on the gun I was framed for the crime. But as I said, the truth came out, and all charges were dropped. I was nowhere near the store that night, but her boyfriend dressed as an Amish man and set me up in retaliation. Still, my part in helping her leave with the gun was inexcusable to the Amish."

Grace frowned. "Yes, well, I can see how possessing a gun would be. Even if it wasn't yours. It's why I left my *daed*'s gun in the closet. It's plain wrong."

Jack wished she would forgive herself for wanting to protect herself, but as long as she continued to allow him to protect her, he was satisfied. "I thought I was helping this girl, if that matters to you."

She lowered her chin and met his gaze from the stair above him. A serene expression softened her blue-green eyes, one that made Jack think maybe his innocence did matter to her. The idea nearly made him take the step up, to be closer to her.

No, he told himself, he was just being silly.

He cleared his throat and refocused on what really mattered. Catching a thief. "I need to call Nic to come get the horse," he said. "You should go in and tend to your father. He needs you."

Grace nodded and turned toward the door. With her hand on the knob, she paused and looked over her shoulder. Only half her face was visible beyond the side of her white *kapp*, but she tilted her head toward him as she said, “By the way, about you helping the girl escape… It does matter…to me.”

The next moment, she slipped inside and closed the door with a soft click.

Jack took in a deep breath that filled his chest with a feeling he hadn’t had in a long time. As he made his way back to the horse trailer, he wrestled with an astounding realization that he never thought possible for himself.

Grace.

She had given him grace.

Grace sat at the table with Benjamin. Together they continued shucking the remaining sweet corn. When Grace grabbed her fourth ear, she smiled at how her *daed* was so meticulous with each strand of wispy silk. He was still on his first ear, and at this rate, the corn would go bad before she was able to preserve the kernels in jars. She finished shucking her ear and placed it on the heaping pyramid.

“How ever did you manage to do all these today?” she asked. “Especially with going into town.” Grace withheld criticizing his slow speed, but couldn’t help taking notice of it.

“That man helped me with the load,” Benjamin replied, his head bent low over the corn as he inspected it.

“Man? Which man?” Grace asked. “Do you mean Sheriff Maddox? The sheriff wasn’t here, *Daed*. He found you in town. You did all the work.”

“I know. I know!” he shouted in frustration, a new behavior for him that stole away more of her hope for his recovery. Slowly, he brought the ear to the perfect triangle of shucked corn. He placed it on top, but in the wrong direction. He pushed it down, trying to keep it in place, but when Grace jumped to her feet to help him right it, she was too late.

Corn began to roll down the sides of the pyramid faster than she could stop them. They tumbled over the table like a rumbling waterfall. Grace gave up the rescue attempt and let them go, instead starting to pick fallen ones up from the floor.

"Here, *Daed.* You can stack them again if you'd like. You did such a good job the first time. I'm sorry they rolled off." She placed a few ears on the table at a time but stopped when she noticed he wasn't piling them again. In fact, he seemed confused as to what to do with them. Grace grabbed a few and lined them up to show him. "Like this, *Daed.* Put them in a line." She did the first row. "Now you do the next row."

Benjamin squinted up at her, and she knew he wasn't placing her at the moment.

"I'm Grace. Your daughter." She sat down and forced a smile on her face. No matter how many times these moments occurred, they still sneaked up on her and hurt just as badly. "Go ahead. You try stacking them," she suggested, but his attempts failed each time. She questioned how he could have forgotten how when he had just piled them so perfectly.

Unless *he* hadn't piled them.

Grace shook the thought away as *ferhoodled.* No man had been here with him. It was his confused mind that made him say that. The sheriff said he had found Benjamin walking alone downtown. No, he had piled these ears fine only a few hours ago.

His dementia was progressing.

Grace was heartbroken at the thought. The doctor had said it would, but he didn't mention it would be this fast. Hank was right. She couldn't leave him alone any longer. He needed to stay with her.

She stacked the next row. "Thank you for your help, *Daed*. You worked hard today. And so fast."

Grace paused as an uneasy feeling overcame her once again. He'd worked too fast, she thought. He couldn't have shucked all the corn by himself.

But who could have helped him?

And if someone had been here, why did they let her *daed* leave and wander into town alone? Or had they taken him there?

Grace struggled to wrap her mind around the idea, just as her father struggled with stacking the corn. Until the kitchen door banged open, startling her from her thoughts. She jumped up and dropped the corn she was holding to the floor, before realizing Jack stood before her.

"*Ach*, it's only you," she said, catching her breath.

"Are you all right?" he asked in a rush, studying her from her head to her toes as he hurried forward. He looked to her *daed*. "Is Benjamin?"

Grace ran her eyes over the scattered ears of corn, but the mess wasn't the problem. It was the image of the perfect pile earlier that sent a shiver up her spine. "Someone's been here. Someone was with *Daed* while we were gone."

Grace expected Jack to laugh at her notion, but instead, he gave a firm nod.

"*Ya*," he said, and swallowed hard. "And they got the horse."

TEN

Jack stood near the front door, waiting for his supervisor to arrive. "Nic should be here any minute." He peered out the side window with his gun in his hand. "Maybe you should take your father upstairs."

"How do you know they're still here?" Grace asked. She stood at the table with a bucket filled with corn. "If they have the horse wouldn't they just leave?"

Jack couldn't believe he had lost the animal after being so careful to keep an eye on him. But right now, losing the thoroughbred was the least of his worries. Grace and Benjamin could have been harmed while under his care. Jack felt sick to his stomach at the thought of how close this person had gotten to them. Was it the same young man who had shot at him? Jack hoped the boy would see the light before it was too late for him. Regardless, whoever it was had been in the house with Benjamin. He had most likely taken him to town and left him there as a message: Next time he might not leave Benjamin or Grace alive.

"No, Grace. They know we are onto them. Nic will be here soon as my backup. I know now this is not a job I can do alone. Benjamin needs protection and I can't give him that while hunting this person or people down."

"I'm not leaving here," Grace said firmly. "This is the only home I've ever known. I have refused to give it up for anybody, and I will not give it up for these thieves." She folded her arms in front of her.

Once again, Jack was reminded of how strong and brave this Amish woman was. Unfortunately, she did not stand a chance against the operation going down around her. "This is not Leroy or Bishop Bontrager we're dealing with," he said. "If these thugs want you gone, you will be taken out."

"Then they must think they can use me, if I'm still here."

"Perhaps you're right." Jack gave her words consideration. He would have to wait until Nic arrived to decide his next steps. "We can plan another trip to the track to purchase another horse. But that will be up to my supervisor to decide. We will have to bring your father with us, because I am not leaving him alone again."

"I'm not, either." She gazed at her *daed* and frowned. Benjamin sat at the table, still shucking the same corn he'd had in his hand when Jack came in the house. Jack hoped he was oblivious to the danger around him. He would allow this man the blissful ignorance instead of the fear.

Grace looked back at him with a determined tilt to her jaw. "Thank you, Jack, for considering my *daed*'s safety."

The sound of crunching gravel in the distance pulled their attention away from Benjamin. Someone was here. Jack waved his hand for Grace to take her father up the stairs. He expected her to follow his orders.

She did not.

With a frustrated sigh, he said, "At least stay low." Jack peered out the window and saw an Amish buggy drawing near. At first he relaxed, but quickly realized he needed to consider all possibilities. Whoever was behind this operation could very well be an Amish person gone rogue.

The buggy pulled up to the side of the house and came to a stop. Jack held his breath as he waited to see who would step out. The setting sun blinded his view through the windshield, and he squinted to try to see through the glass. A few moments later the small door opened, and the hem of a purple dress appeared as a black boot stepped off the buggy.

"It's an Amish woman," he said over his shoulder. "Is it someone you know?"

Grace rushed forward to cut in front of Jack and peer out the window. "I've never seen that person in my life, but that's not unusual. We sell horses. Amish people come from many communities to place orders. That's certain sure why she's here." Grace reached for the doorknob, but Jack shot out a hand and held the door closed.

Grace startled at his move. "It's an Amish woman. I have to answer."

Jack held his gun at the ready. "I'll stand right behind the door. Don't open it all the way. Just enough to welcome her and find out what she wants."

At Grace's nod of compliance, he stepped back so as to remain hidden with his gun drawn. The Amish woman wouldn't understand why he had a weapon out—and he wasn't putting it away. Not when the horse thief could still be out there.

Her first step on the wooden porch galvanized his focus, and he tightened his grip on the gun, his trigger finger itching. Then he slowly let the breath out of his lungs and whispered, "Now," giving Grace the nod to open the door to their visitor.

She pulled the door in, saying, "*Hallo, gut* day. How can I help you?"

"Hallo," a kind woman's voice replied. Kind, but familiar. Jack tried to place it. He thought he knew it, but he had to be wrong. It couldn't be, *could it*? "I'm here about a horse," she continued, this time losing the Amish dialect.

Instantly, Jack recognized the speaker and stepped around the door to confirm what he thought.

"I don't believe it," he said, as he searched the face with a white *kapp* surrounding it.

A smile grew on the visitor's face as she looked him up and down. "I could say the same thing." She glanced to her left and to her right. "Are you going to let me in or keep me a sitting duck out here?" she whispered.

Jack placed a hand on Grace's shoulder. "She's safe. It's my supervisor, Nic Harrington."

Grace stepped back and opened the door wider. "Nic?" she said.

"Nicole, but I go by Nic. You were probably expecting a man. I get that a lot."

Grace blushed. "I apologize. I shouldn't have assumed. I know how it feels. Please come in."

Nic quickly moved inside and shut the door behind

her. "I came as soon as I could make myself inconspicuous. I didn't want to kill your cover." She nodded at Jack and smiled. "Man, you would have had me fooled." She leaned close and squinted at his hair. "Did you glue extensions on?"

"I made a hair piece extension string to go around the back of my head and wove the ends into my own hair at my temples."

"Brilliant. It looks so natural on you. You look so… Amish." She touched her own fiery red hair styled in a neat braid. "Much better than me."

"Don't get used to it," Jack warned. "As soon as I catch these guys, I'm changing back to my old self."

"Are you sure this isn't your old self?" Nic winked Grace's way as though they shared the joke.

Jack didn't play along but led them into the kitchen. He caught Grace frowning at him as he turned and wondered what he'd said to affect her like that. But with other pressing matters, he let it go and admitted his failure. "Another horse is gone. Taken this afternoon."

"Are you kidding me?" his supervisor asked, sounding irritated. "How could you let this happen?"

"It wasn't his fault," Grace interjected, wringing her hands together. "Someone took my *daed*, and the sheriff came by to return him. The horse was hidden in the trailer, but the thief used the time we were all out front to steal it."

Nic pursed her lips while she listened to events that suddenly sounded like a setup. She raised an eyebrow his way. "And you fell for it? You're slipping. Has the slow life affected your brain?"

Jack glanced at Grace for a moment before shaking his head. "Not at all. I'm able to do my job. Don't worry about me." He reached for the end of her braid and lifted it. A bright pink elastic held the hair together. "I would say you're slipping too. That's mighty flashy for the Amish."

"Hardly the same." She pulled her braid from his fingers. "You lost a thoroughbred you were supposed to be guarding. What else will you lose?"

Jack supposed he had that coming from his boss. "It won't happen again."

"Of course not. The horse is gone." Nic crossed her arms in front of her. She wore a pristine white apron over her purple dress, so different from her usual blue pantsuit. He didn't let the Amish clothes fool him. Like himself, he knew she packed heat and probably a few knives under her garments.

"Now that you're here, I can dive deep into this investigation without concern for protecting Benjamin and Grace. I'm thinking I can catch the thieves in another theft."

Nic nodded firmly and said, "All right, I'm listening. What's your plan?"

He outlined the plan he'd been working on. "I'll return to Autumn Woods on Tuesday. They'll be testing the horses on the track. I'll bid on another horse. The heists have been lucrative, so the chance of them trying at least one more switch is good. When they give me the wrong horse, I'll know right away who swapped the animals, and get my lead into who to investigate."

"What makes you think they'll try this on you?" Nic asked. She sent Grace a look over her shoulder, "No offense, Ms. Miller, but you're an easy target."

"Then I'll go," Grace offered.

"No," Jack said in an instant. He cringed at his forceful order. When her eyebrows raised in shock, he fumbled for a valid excuse. "It's not safe," he tried to explain. "If things go south, they won't think twice about hurting you. I can't guard you *and* catch these thieves."

Grace took swift steps forward, practically stomping across the kitchen. "What makes you think I need guarding? I can handle myself. I don't need anyone to help me do my job, and I don't need anyone telling me what to do. Let me remind you that it was *you* who lost the horse, not me."

Nic snorted out a short laugh "Grace has got a point, Kaufman. I say let her do her job, and you stand back and observe. Tuesday you'll head back to Autumn Woods together, and you'll stay out of her way, got it?"

Jack felt his blood pressure skyrocket. This was not how he did things. "I work alone. You know that, Nic."

"Not this time," she said, and turned to Benjamin. She took the seat beside him and picked up an ear of corn to shuck. When Jack didn't move from his spot, she glanced up and sent him a look of authority, effective despite the demure Amish *kapp*. "And that's an order."

Carrying a glowing lantern out the back door, Grace wondered where Jack had gone after dinner. He hadn't spoken to her since his boss had arrived. He'd answered Nic's questions at the table, but Grace could tell it was only because he had to. Left to his own choices, they wouldn't have seen him then, either. He probably would have left the farm completely if it hadn't been for Nic's arrival. With the horse gone there really was no reason for him to stay.

But now he'd been ordered to.

Grace stepped into the barn and lifted the lantern to hang on the peg by Peanut's stall. She reached for the pitchfork and opened the door, speaking low to the horse. "Good evening, Peanut. I'm sorry I'm so late today. So much has gone on, I can't comprehend it. But things should get back to normal soon."

"That's what you think," a voice muttered from the barn's back door.

Grace gave a start, but even in the shadowy lantern light she could tell it was Jack's looming silhouette in the doorway.

He took a few steps inside and said, "You shouldn't be out here. It's still not safe." He walked over to the lantern and, before she knew what he planned, blew it out, leaving them in total darkness. "We don't need to make ourselves a target. Your pitchfork won't stop a bullet."

Grace dropped her gaze to the pitchfork in her hands. Slowly, she placed it against the stall, saying, "Do you really think someone is still out there? They have what they came for. Why would they stay? They could get caught."

Jack huffed. "Only if you can identify them. And only if they let you live."

She jerked her head up. She couldn't see his face clearly, but his remarks told her he thought she was naive—and still in danger.

Jack moved closer until only a foot separated them.

She inhaled sharply as he neared. Moonlight filtering through the opened doors glinted in his stern eyes. His frown worried her and caused a bit of unease to settle in.

She kept her head high and said, "If you're trying to scare me into staying home, it won't work."

Their gazes met in a match of wills. Who would back down? She took a deep breath and resigned herself for the long haul.

It seemed moments later when Jack gave in. "I'm sorry," he said, reaching for her forearm. She thought she should pull away, but couldn't even if she wanted to.

If he hadn't caved, she was certain sure she would have, very soon.

His grip tightened, more and more with each passing second. It was almost as if he was testing the limits of their closeness. "I shouldn't have been so blunt. It's just that I've seen this ugly side of the world that you haven't. You can't fathom how dangerous some individuals are. Money does horrible things to people, and the idea of such ugliness touching you…" Jack swallowed hard and seemed to be struggling to voice what consumed his mind.

She placed a gentle hand over his where he gripped her arm. Slowly, he released her, but she kept her hand there, keeping him close. "I know you think I don't understand the danger, but I want you to know I do."

His head tilted. A sad but frustrated look crossed his shadowed face. His gaze sharpened on her as he asked, "Then why would you agree to go back to the racetrack? If you understand the danger, why would you put yourself through it?"

Grace lifted her chin and licked her lips before pressing them together. With a sigh, she simply said, "Because to not go would cost me more."

Jack stood before her in a silence that lingered, until he dropped his head with a nod. "I understand. I wish it wasn't so, but I can't change the Amish ways any more now than I could when I was eighteen. Leaving was my only choice."

"Leaving is never a choice," she said. "Not for me, and it wasn't for you, either. You just thought it was."

"You don't know what you're talking about." He started to pull away, but this time she gripped him tightly, keeping him close when she sensed he would retreat.

"Then tell me." She locked her gaze on his frantic stare. "What happened to make you think leaving was your only choice?"

"Simple. I wasn't worthy to be Amish."

Grace couldn't challenge the absurdity of that statement. How many times had she felt inadequate as an Amish woman? She was expected to marry and have *kinner*. But she was also here to serve her community. "I know living up to what the Amish *ordnung* expects of us can lead to feelings of shame when our choices don't match, but that doesn't make us unworthy. It means we may need to remember why we committed to living the Amish way in the first place."

"That's the problem. I guess I forgot why when my own family turned their backs on me. Why would I want to remember a way of life that approves of such treatment to one of their own?"

Grace found herself balancing on a tightrope, with

drastic consequences if she said the wrong thing. She couldn't say she had never worried what might happen to her if she continued to disregard Leroy's aspirations to marry her. Bishop Bontrager had made it known that she couldn't put Leroy off for much longer.

She bit her lower lip, searching for the words, then said, "I understand. But I also know there are times we all must do things we don't want to in order to protect our Amish ways. These ideals are put in place not to hurt us but to bring peace."

"But what if you know in your heart that you must take a stand? What if your life depends on it? Or someone else's? Wouldn't you rather be truthful than live a lie?"

Grace swallowed hard, now wobbling on that high wire. "I don't know what you mean," she said lamely.

"Yes, you do." Jack's eyes hardened, and he seemed to be closer than he had been a moment ago. Had he moved in?

Grace stood firm and returned his determined look. She didn't know what his purpose was for showing aggression, but she wouldn't allow it. "How so?" she asked with pursed lips.

"You're a fighter, Grace. Whether you want to admit it or not."

"I am not. It's wrong to *fechde*."

"There are other ways to fight than with your hands. You can also fight with your heart. Tell me, how long did you hold off Leroy's marriage proposal?"

Grace sighed and dropped her chin a bit. Guilt swamped her at being called to task for going against the wishes of Bishop Bontrager. She'd known for a long time that marriage was what the elders wanted for her. And without her parents able to care for her and direct her, it was the elders who stepped in to fill that role.

"Five years," she said, unable to keep the note of shame from her voice.

She felt Jack touch under her chin, but she refused to look him in the eye. She glanced through her lashes to find him now only inches from her. A thought to retreat entered her mind. She should bolt, as fast as possible. She questioned his motives and wondered if he meant to kiss her. The idea of such liberties shocked her. Except a part of her also wondered what it would be like—something she never wondered with Leroy.

Grace swallowed hard. "Why are you doing this?" she whispered.

"I keep asking myself the same question. For some reason I care. I can't explain it. All I know is that I see the injustice going on around you and it stirs something in me. I see you fighting for your place in this community, and maybe I wish I had fought for mine. Instead, I ran. I let their words push me away." He huffed. "Believe it or not, you're much braver than I ever was."

She frowned. "You seeing this in me only makes me feel guiltier."

He applied enough pressure to lift her head up and force her to meet his gaze. "You have nothing to feel guilty about. You have so much responsibility and have taken it all in stride."

"I did what was expected of me."

"No." His eyes pierced straight into her. "What was expected of you was to marry and hand over your profession to someone else, but deep down you know you are the best person for this job. You know Leroy would fall short, and you know the horses would suffer at his hands. You know your *daed*'s lifelong work and his *daed*'s would be ruined. You didn't do what was expected of you, you did what was needed. Even if it meant you did it alone and without the elders' blessing."

Grace felt her lungs tighten, and she realized she hadn't taken a breath since Jack lifted her face to his. No matter how much she needed air, she stood motionless, riveted by his examination of her. How could he know her innermost thoughts? She'd never shared them with anyone. Suddenly, she could see what made this ex-Amish man a *gut* lawman.

"Your investigative skills are thorough," she said, as she finally breathed deep.

"Does that mean you'll stay away from Autumn Woods and let me handle the horse purchases from now on?"

Grace jumped back, instantly seeing where Jack had been going in his estimation of her. Her hand hit the pitchfork she had placed against the wall, and her fingers curled around it. "That's what this is about? You came in here to get me to concede to your wishes, by praising me for not conceding to Bishop Bontrager's?"

Pivoting, Grace picked up the pitchfork and returned to the job of mucking out Peanut's stall. In a rush, she whacked at the hay and pulled it into a pile. A feeling came over her that she had never experienced and couldn't name even if she tried.

"Grace, stop." Jack's hands covered hers. "Look at me."

She tried to continue forking up the hay, but Jack's strength was no match, no matter how angry she felt.

Anger?

Was that what she was feeling? But why? She hadn't even felt anger when her *mamm* died. What had changed in her to bring it out now?

"I didn't mean to upset you." Jack held her still. She could barely see his face inside the dim stall and hoped he couldn't see hers.

Especially when she felt tears begin to well up in her eyes. Squeezing them to stop any flow, she took another deep breath and said in a steady voice, "I'm going to Autumn Woods, and you can't stop me."

"Please, just hear me out." He sounded exasperated. But then so was she.

She pulled away to go back to mucking. "So you can explain why I should follow your orders when you don't follow your own boss's?" She jabbed hard.

"Nic is wrong. She's thinking this is only a horse theft operation. Sometimes things aren't as they seem. I really believe we are dealing with something much more sinister, and for some reason, someone has targeted you to take the fall. Or worse."

She swiped the fork at the growing pile. "Since you're FBI and know I didn't steal any horses, I'm not worried. If framing me is their plan, they won't succeed. I won't take the fall for any crime, because you know I'm innocent."

"I said 'or worse.'" Jack's voice held such an ominous note that she stopped jabbing at the hay. "Do you understand what I'm saying to you, Grace? If something happened to you, I would never forgive myself."

She turned her head to look into his shadowed face, and took a step closer. "I'm just buying a horse. It will be like any other day at the track. I will be careful and on the lookout for any potential danger. And you will be there to point out any that you see."

He dropped his head with a sigh. "What if I miss something, like today with the horse?"

Grace suddenly realized what this was all about. She felt *ferhoodled* for thinking Jack had been planning to kiss her. He was only feeling guilty for missing the thief earlier. She felt suddenly let down.

Shaking the absurdity away, she touched his arm in the dark and said, "That was not your fault. They used my *daed* to trick us."

He leaned so close she could see the whites of his eyes. "That fact should scare you enough to stay home. If they would use Benjamin for their purposes, what else would they do to get what they wanted?"

With that, he turned abruptly and left her alone in the barn. But even as she finished up and headed back to the house, she knew he hadn't gone far. He was nearby, keeping watch over her.

Grace couldn't explain the feeling, but she sensed there was a connection between them, and oddly, she found it comforting. He hadn't expected her to hand over the pitchfork, but instead he'd given her the space to work, all the while standing by in case she needed him.

Grace prayed she wouldn't.

ELEVEN

A gunshot blasted through the air and jolted Jack's already heightened senses. Even as a single horse with its cart and driver attached set off on its time trial, he scanned the crowd for the lingering threat waiting to take a more lethal shot. This was the tenth trial Jack had watched since he and Grace had arrived at Autumn Woods on Tuesday morning. Most racetracks installed starting gates, but this small ranch went old-school, with a starter pistol fired off in the air. Jack figured it would be a perfect opportunity for his bad guy to shoot a loaded gun without anyone being the wiser. At least until the bullet found its mark.

And by then it would be too late…for Grace.

Jack grumbled at her decision to be at the ranch today and straightened to full alert. He narrowed his gaze at the crowd of spectators and bidders. Unlike the last time, the track bustled this morning, with dozens of visitors, and a long line of horses at the hitching posts, harnessed to their racing carts and ready for their test run. Jack leaned back against the track fence and surveyed the area for any suspicious characters and interactions. So far all seemed legit, but with the horse thefts and shootouts, he knew that to be a facade.

From where he stood he had a clear, unobstructed view of where Grace sat in the stands. She had been so excited to wear her own boots today. Her feet were healing well. He smiled and glanced her way now—and nearly caught his breath, seeing her enthralled expression as she scrutinized the latest horse flying down the track.

Regardless of the fact that she was a sitting target, she was the best person for this job, he thought. She knew what she was looking for in a good horse, but she also appreciated the power and beauty of the star equines.

As the speeding horse ran by her, Jack watched Grace reach for the strings of her *kapp* and pull them down. Again, he wondered what made her do it. He'd seen her grab hold of them before, and had thought it was something she did when she was afraid. But what could be frightening her now? Did she see a threatening person? Jack turned to follow the direction of her gaze, expecting to find danger, but saw only the horse.

Perhaps it wasn't fear at all that instigated her string-pulling habit.

She bit her lip as the horse came around the curve and crossed the finish line directly in front of her. She looked up at the clock and smiled brightly. Jack followed her gaze to the timing results and thought it strange that she smiled. The horse wasn't nearly as fast as the two previous ones.

She let go of her *kapp* straps and raised a hand.

One of the ranch staff walked over to the bleachers

and called up to her. At her nod, he ripped off a slip of paper from his clipboard and climbed the steps. Grace counted out cash and handed it over in exchange for the paper. Once the man was back on the track, she searched the crowd, and Jack lifted a hand so she could spot him. With a straight face, she held up the slip and nodded once. The deed was done.

She had just purchased a horse.

Jack waited for Grace to make her way to him. So far, things were moving smoothly. They would soon know if the thief planned to use her again to swap a thoroughbred out of the stable in place of the horse she'd just bought. If the thief didn't know she had figured out what was going on, whoever it was just might attempt another exchange.

The starting pistol signaled another horse trial, jolting Jack as he waited for Grace to reach him. She was at the top of the track near the gate now. The next horse was already there, awaiting its turn. Grace stopped to pet the animal's nose, then Jack saw a man dressed in a white shirt and blue jeans step down from the cart. He approached the other side of the horse and met Grace with a word and a smile. From this distance, Jack couldn't tell what they talked about, but after a few minutes, she nodded and climbed into the cart.

Suddenly, Jack had a feeling something wasn't normal. Why was Grace taking the reins?

Unsure what was happening, he walked briskly around the curved fence, doing his best not to bring attention to himself as she moved the horse inside the gate. Seeing an Amish man running would raise some heads, and so would calling out to her. Jack pressed his lips tight—until the gun went off and Grace shot forward on the track.

Now he picked up his pace and raced toward the opening, yelling, "Grace! No!" His eyes stayed on the back of her *kapp* as she brought the horse around the first bend. In his peripheral vision, he caught sight of the man who had relinquished the cart and horse to her.

"What were you thinking?" Jack shouted, running up to him.

"About what?" the man asked, lifting his attention from a clipboard in his hand.

"Why did you let her take the horse?" Jack couldn't control his breathing as fear set in. "She could get hurt." He ripped his straw hat off his head and almost reached for his hair, suddenly remembering his disguise but not really caring at the moment. All he cared about was Grace's safety. He tore his gaze from her to search the crowd. Would someone take their shot now?

Suddenly the man beside him started to chuckle, then laugh. "Buddy," he said with a shake of his head, "I think you've got it bad for that young woman."

"What?" Jack shot him a heated glare. How dare he say such a thing? But Jack could only think of Grace, currently driving like the wind on the racetrack. "Get her back here now," he ordered.

The jeans-clad man checked the stopwatch he held in his other hand. "I'd say give her about thirty more seconds, and she'll drive the horse back in. That's usually her time. Although this is Game Changer she's racing, so it might be sooner."

"Usually?" The word tumbled from Jack's lips.

The man let out another laugh and pointed at the

track. "Grace has been coming here with her father her whole life. Every now and then, she gives a horse a run. It's our little secret." He lifted a finger to his lips.

"The Amish race their buggies. It's not taboo."

"Even the women?" the man asked with raised eyebrows.

Jack paused. The answer was most likely no, and as he saw Grace take the next bend, back toward them, he watched her face as she neared at breakneck speed. As she closed in on the finish line, she flicked the reins harder and faster, wearing a huge smile the likes of which he'd never seen on her. She looked free to be herself and was clearly enjoying every second.

"Has she ever slowed down just to make the ride a little longer?" Jack asked.

"Doubtful. That's not Grace's style. She puts her best foot forward and cuts no corners." The man stretched out a hand. "I'm Steven Byler."

"Nice to meet you." Jack grasped it firmly. "Steven. You work in the stables, right?"

He nodded. "For my whole adult life, yup."

The two men watched Grace drive the cart over the finish line and then pull on the reins for the slowdown. As she passed Jack, she lifted her hand to wave.

But in the next second, a loud snap echoed through the arena, and her face lost its smile. The reins were ripped from her hands as the horse veered away.

Grace let out a shriek as she and the cart continued on at a high speed, before turning and flipping over.

Jack watched in disbelief as the cart bounced and flipped again, sending Grace into the air. Her cries of fear spurred his legs to move. She landed hard against the ground, and though his arms reached out as he ran, he couldn't get there in time to break her fall.

His boots pounded on the packed dirt as he rushed toward where she lay in the grass of the center ring.

"Grace!" he yelled but received no response.

"An ambulance is on the way!" Steven called from behind, a cell phone in his hand.

Jack didn't dare move her but dropped to the ground at her side. "Please, Grace, answer me if you hear me." He touched his fingertips to her cheek and then the side of her neck.

A fast pulse bounced under his touch.

Even so, Jack rushed out a prayer. "*Gött,* I don't expect much for myself, but Grace loves You and lives for You. Could You please let her live through this? Please protect her. I don't know what I'll do if..." Jack choked on the words, not able to utter them. He swallowed hard, reasoning that his concern was only because she was in his charge. He pushed aside the fear of finding out if he was wrong and it was something else entirely. Something that was impossible.

Jack avoided the whole idea of Grace being more than a job and turned an ear to hear Steven talking to the dispatcher. The stable hand was relaying details of the accident over the phone. Jack understood only bits and pieces, until he heard him say, "The cart came unhitched from the horse. I don't understand. I attached it myself. This has never happened before."

Jack couldn't take his gaze off Grace's unconscious form, but his mind spun Steven's words around and around until they finally made sense.

This has never happened before.

As sirens wailed in the distance, Jack knew the thing he feared most today had come to fruition. His plan to catch a thief had been turned on him, as quickly as Grace had taken the curves around the track. The smooth transaction he had hoped for had turned deadly, and Jack knew beyond a doubt that someone had their own plans for Grace.

Plans to kill her.

A beeping sound stirred Grace awake, but when she tried to turn her head toward the noise, something stopped any movement. Panic set in and she opened her eyes, to find herself staring straight up at a white ceiling. Dim lighting cast shadows on as much of the cream-colored walls as she could see without moving her head. The incessant beeping picked up its pace as she struggled to figure out where she was. All she knew was that this was not her home.

"Hello, Miss Miller," a male voice said. Then a face peered over her—no one she knew, but he appeared to be a medical professional.

"Am I in the hospital?" she asked, though barely any sound came out.

"Yes, you are. I'm Dr. Reese, and we've been waiting for you to come to before taking you out of traction."

"Tr-traction?" She had no idea what he meant, having never been in the hospital.

"It's like a brace, so you don't hurt herself by moving too much."

"But why?" Nothing made sense.

"Do you remember being in an accident?"

Grace tried to shake her head, then remembered she couldn't. "Did a car hit my buggy?"

Dr. Reese smiled. "Nope. You were racing a horse at the track. Do you remember that? The cart came detached and flipped, and you were knocked unconscious. Anything coming back to you?"

"No," she said, but did her best to remember. Suddenly, an image of the beautiful horse Game Changer entered her mind. "Wait. Steven Byler asked me if I wanted to test Game Changer." Fear rushed to the forefront of her mind. "Is the horse all right? Please tell me she is okay."

"Game Changer? Is that the horse's name?"

"Yes. Is she safe?"

"As far as I know, she is fine. She ran off and left you and the cart behind. But I'm glad to hear you remember some things from the event. It tells me your memory is intact. I think you'll be on the mend real soon. Your X-rays came back clean, but you'll be sore for a while. Your neck especially needs to remain stable. You'll go home wearing a brace, until the muscles and ligaments heal. But you have some wonderful people in your community ready to help. In fact, I have someone out in the waiting room itching to see you. Are you all right with that?"

Grace figured the person waiting had to be Jack. "*Ya*, please send him in." She was eager to see him and wished she could sit up. There was so much to ask him. Had he picked up the horse she'd bought? Had it been swapped for a thoroughbred? There were so many questions, but also another feeling she couldn't describe. An eagerness to see Jack that went beyond a working relationship. But that couldn't be, she told herself. She was just scared and in need of some comfort right now. Still, she couldn't imagine it coming from anyone else.

As the doctor exited and she waited for Jack, the beeping on the machine slowed back to its former pace. Knowing he had come to the hospital for her offered her the comfort she needed in this unfamiliar place. She hoped he could bring her home tonight. She was thankful Nic was with her *daed*, but she still needed to be home with him. Grace closed her eyes and sighed at the thought, and when she heard footsteps enter the door, she felt her stomach do a little flip, knowing he was near.

A swishing sound met her ears, followed by the feel of a strong hand taking hers and squeezing. She had hoped for warmth but found it cold to the touch.

"I'm surprised to see you awake," a hushed male voice said.

But not Jack's voice.

Grace tensed up in her prostrate position. As she pressed her face to the right to try and see who stood beside her, the beeping on the machine picked back up. She realized it represented the beating of her heart, which was now pounding in her chest.

"Who are you?" she asked, trying to pull her hand away. "Let me see your face."

The man's grip held fast and hard. "You really shouldn't be racing horses, Grace. That is not becoming behavior for a good Amish woman. What would the elders say? What will they do with you when you have already given them so much to be concerned about?"

Grace whimpered as she tried to see out the corner

of her eye, but the man stood at the top of the bed, just out of view. Trying to pull her hand away did nothing but bring on a tighter, more painful grasp.

"You're hurting me," she said. "Let me go! Help! Someone, help!"

A sick laugh erupted beside her. It stopped just as quickly as it started, then he said, "You don't belong with the Amish. In fact, you shouldn't have ever been born. I think it's time for you to go away."

"Help!" She yelled as loudly as she could, forcing a scream past the raspy sounds that escaped her lips. She opened them again, but before she could call out once more, a pillow came down over her face.

Grace realized in disbelief what was happening but couldn't move a muscle to avoid the pillow that was pressing down. She screamed into the plush cotton and fought against the traction, trying to turn her head even a fraction of an inch. Anything to avoid having her life snuffed out of her.

It was no use. And with each passing second, the air in her lungs dispersed, leaving a deep ache behind. Bright flashes of light beneath her eyelids blinded her as unconsciousness closed in. Her free hand reached for the pillow to try to pull it away. She gripped the cotton then fumbled for her assailant's hand on the pillow.

She felt her hand go still, with no more energy left in her. Darkness won out over the bright, explosive lights. Her other hand went limp in her attacker's tight hold.

Who are you?

That final thought filled her mind as she gave in to escape the pain and stopped struggling.

She floated in that dark, unconscious world between

life and death. Silence filled her ears for what seemed an eternity, and then, as if through a tunnel, she detected the familiar beeping sound filtering in, slowly at first, then picking up speed.

She thought she heard a swishing sound, but suddenly the pain racketing through her chest stole her attention. Her body involuntarily worked to fill her lungs with air.

Which meant the pillow was gone.

Gasping, Grace forced her eyes wide, to find the white ceiling again. But this time Jack's worried face leaned over her. His hands grabbed at her cheeks and his lips moved. He was speaking to her. Slowly, his voice registered, and she realized he was yelling for help.

Then the swishing sound came again, and Jack was gone from her view. Dr. Reese replaced him, his hands touching her and lifting her eyelids.

"Grace, can you hear me?" he asked.

She couldn't nod or speak. She mouthed *"yes"* and hoped that came out right. Saying someone had tried to kill her seemed impossible, but they needed to know. She mouthed, *"Kill. Pillow."*

Dr. Reese's eye widened. He looked behind him and said, "I think she's trying to say 'kill.'" He glanced her way again. "Is that right?"

"Pillow," she whispered.

Jack spoke from somewhere in the room. "I resuscitated her when I came in and saw her flatlined. But I didn't know someone had suffocated her with a pillow. He must have just left before I came in." Jack sounded angry. “Don’t leave her side until I get back. He can’t be far.”

The swishing sound occurred again, and Grace realized now it was the door to her room opening and closing.

Dr. Reese continued his examination, but Grace barely focused on him. She wished she could see the door. But if her attacker came back, she wouldn’t know him. She hadn’t seen his face. It could be anyone. He could walk right back in and try again.

“Your friend’s quick work of resuscitating you saved your life,” the doctor said, grabbing her attention at last with those words.

Jack had saved her?

But from whom? Grace licked her dry lips. She clasped her hands together in front of her, rubbing the blood back into her fingers and flexing them to ease the pain from where her attacker had squeezed so tightly.

She tried to remember the sound of the man’s voice. Was it someone she knew?

The swishing sound came again.

“Keep the door open,” Dr. Reese said. “Who closed that, anyway?”

A nurse appeared to assist the doctor. She checked Grace’s vitals as Grace tried to remember how many times she had heard that sound. The first time was when her attacker entered the room. He must have shut the door. Then she’d heard him leave, and the other two times were Jack coming in and going out.

Would he find the man? Grace wanted this whole thing to be over and done with. She wanted to go home to her father and her horses and Jack.

The last thought stumped her. Jack was not part of her life. It was wrong of her to think such things. Jack wasn't a possibility in her life. But just then, he walked back in and went to the bottom of her bed so she could see him. His breathing was labored, as though he'd been running. "Nothing," he said. "Who was it?" His gaze pierced her with anger.

But not anger aimed at her.

Grace knew he was mad at himself for not keeping her safe.

"I don't know. He wouldn't let me see his face. He sounded so mean. Almost like he was glad I was hurt. And he said I should leave the Amish."

When Jack didn't respond, Grace searched his face for the truth. "Tell me what you're thinking."

"I'm thinking that botched horse trial was no accident. It was set up for you to take the reins. And when they failed in killing you there, they tried to finish the job here. Now do you see how dangerous this is?"

"B-but that's not possible. How would they know I would race her? Steven had brought her out to the lineup."

"Did Steven ask you to race Game Changer? Or did you ask?"

Grace focused as hard as she could, but her mind was still muddled. An ache was also starting to form in her head to match the one in her chest. Whatever medication they must have given her for pain was wearing off. "I remember petting the horse. I think Steven came down off the cart and mentioned that they needed a driver. I'm light enough and sometimes I take the horses out."

"But did he ask you specifically?"

Grace tried to nod her head as the conversation came back, but she was immovable. "*Ya*, he asked me to drive the cart."

"Then it was Steven who tried to kill you." Jack's jaw clenched and anger glittered in his eyes.

Grace's throat closed at such a malevolent statement. All she could squeak out was, "Kill?"

In the next second, heavy footsteps came into the room, just like the ones she'd heard when her attacker entered, and Grace let out a bloodcurdling scream.

TWELVE

Jack spun around to come face-to-face with Hank Maddox. The sheriff sent him a scathing look before approaching a hysterical Grace in her hospital bed. When Hank pushed past him, Jack fought the urge to grab the man's arm and yank him away from her, but right now, he needed him. There was a dangerous criminal on the loose who was after Grace.

"Grace, it's only me," Hank said as he leaned over her. "I came as soon as I heard what happened." He held her hand and gave her comfort as he spoke soothingly to her. Slowly, her cries subsided.

"Sheriff?" Grace's raspy voice squeaked. "I thought you were him."

"Who?" Sheriff Maddox asked.

"The man who tried to kill me. He was in my room," she said frantically. "I couldn't do anything. I need to get out of this brace."

He patted her hand. "I'll see what I can do. But right now I need to know, did you get a look at this person?"

"No, not at all. He kept himself hidden, and I couldn't turn because of the brace. And then the pillow was all I could see." Her voice cracked with tears that made Jack fist his hands in anger. "Jack says the accident at the track was also done on purpose, to kill me."

Hank glanced at Jack over his shoulder with a disgusted expression. "That might not be accurate."

Jack crossed his arms in front of his chest. "I have to disagree. I've seen enough crime scenes to know foul play was involved."

Hank's eyes narrowed. "And how does an Amish man find himself at crime scenes? Please, enlighten me, Mr. Kaufman. Were they your own crimes?"

Jack clamped his back teeth together to keep from giving up any more of his cover. "I've been around."

Hank straightened up. "Yeah, you should know I'm looking into the places you've been around. I'd like to know where you've been hiding out for eight years. It's like you've vanished off the face of the earth after you left your Colorado community."

"Nope, I'm right here." That was all Jack was giving the guy.

"I'd like to know why you didn't do time."

"Because, like I told you before, all charges were dropped. I was innocent."

"Does she know what you did yet? If you're not going to tell her, I will."

Grace pulled at Hank's hand. "Yes, he has, but I don't care. He's been helpful to me and *Daed*. Just like you have been. I need you to accept this."

"So that's it?" Hank tugged his hand away. "You're going to take the word of a stranger over my warning just because he is Amish? Amelia, you're making a big mistake."

"Amelia?" Jack said.

"I mean Grace," Hank amended quickly. "It's been a trying night, sorry."

"Grace's *mamm* Amelia?" Jack asked.

"It was a slip. They look so much alike, is all."

"It doesn't matter," Grace interjected with a frown. "What matters is you can't tell me I'm making a mistake. I will take Jack's word that he was innocent of all charges. He's been through enough."

Hank's face flushed, but Grace had set things straight with him on where she stood on the subject, and there was nothing the man could do about it.

"I stopped to inform your father of your accident," he announced after a pause. "Benjamin was with an Amish woman I've never seen before. Another long-lost relative?" he asked Grace point-blank.

Her gaze shifted to Jack and her lips pressed closed. Jack was glad she didn't blow Nic's cover.

Hank huffed in annoyance. "That's what I thought. There's something going on around here, and I will figure it out." He turned to leave, but Jack put a hand on his chest to stop him as he tried to brush by.

Jack locked gazes with the sheriff. "Someone tried to kill Grace today. That cart was tampered with, and I had to resuscitate her after someone attempted to smother her right here in the hospital. There's something else more pressing going on around here than me and my past. Don't waste your time with me, or Grace could end up paying for it with her life. Do your job and find the man who came in here. There must be surveillance in the halls, at least. But I would start with the stable hands, if I were you."

"Well, you're not." Hank sneered and grabbed Jack's hand to throw it off him. "But Steven Byler is in the waiting room, so I'll go talk to him now. For all I know, *you* did this."

Once Hank stormed from the room, Jack stood in silence, thinking about his next move in protecting Grace and catching a horse thief.

"You have to tell him you're undercover," Grace said. "It's not right for me to lie."

He walked to the foot of her bed and faced her. "You haven't lied at all, and I will never make you. If there comes a time you feel there is no other answer but the truth, you have my permission."

"*Denki*." Her eyelids drooped down, and he knew she needed rest. But as he made a move to go sit outside her room, Grace's eyes shot open. "No, don't go. Please don't leave me alone."

He grabbed her hand, rubbing his thumb over hers. Just moments before, Hank had held her hand the same way. It was such an intimate display, and yet Grace accepted it without complaint.

Jack figured Hank had to be at least thirty years older than Grace, and as the sheriff, he shouldn't have such a close relationship with the Amish. It went against the social norm of separation from the English, and especially from law enforcement.

Her hand curled in his, and their fingers locked in a clasp. He took a deep breath and asked, "Does Hank treat all the Amish like he treats you?"

"No..." Grace's words slurred as her eyes drifted shut again. "He cares for me."

Jack frowned, then expelled a rush of air as though

she'd sucker-punched him. "He's English," Jack sputtered. There were so many other valid reasons for such a relationship to be taboo, but that was the only one to form on his tongue.

"It's not what you think," Grace said. "Hank was my *mamm*'s friend."

Her response stumped him as he tried to understand how this could be. After a few moments, Jack realized there was only one way. Hank wasn't an Amish man, so that could only mean… "Your *mamm* was English?" he asked.

But Grace didn't respond, and one look showed she had fallen fast asleep. Jack refrained from shaking her awake. He had so many questions that needed answers, but he wouldn't be getting them tonight. Tonight, he would stand guard over this woman who just might be in danger because of something other than her expertise with horses. It was too bad Amelia was no longer alive to shed some light on her past.

But perhaps there was a reason Grace's *mamm* was already dead, and that reason was more than a loud car and a spooked horse.

Grace's ears vibrated from the loud noise. She whimpered where she lay in the grass, knowing her *mamm* was only a few feet away, hurt…or worse. But no matter how hard Grace tried to move, her body wouldn't budge. She cried out for her mother again, "*Mamm*, please tell me you're all right. *Mamm,* answer me, *please*!"

"Grace! Grace!" a male voice called to her from somewhere far off.

She searched the blue sky above, but not a face could be seen. Grace tried to look around the open field where her body had been thrown from the buggy but couldn't turn her head. No matter how hard she tried, her face stayed straight in place, staring up to the sky.

"Grace, wake up!" the voice came again.

She recognized it and was instantly frantic to find him. "Jack!" she called out. "Jack, help me!"

"I'm right here, *lieb.* Open your eyes. I'm right in front of you. I've got you, love."

Confusion set in and suddenly the blue sky was swapped out for bright lights that blinded her as she gazed at the face above her. The very one she needed to see in this heart-wrenching moment of losing her mother all over again.

But the electric lights were so bright she had to close her eyes again until she could adjust to the glare.

"It was just a dream," Jack said. "It wasn't real."

Tears pooled in her eyes. He was wrong. It was very real. Grace tried to shake her head back and forth, then remembered why she was locked in place. The unforgiving traction bound her to the bed and kept her from reinjuring herself. But she needed Jack to know he was wrong.

"It was real," she insisted, reaching out for him. "Or at least parts of it. There was one part that I'm not sure of. It all happened so fast. I don't know what it means."

Jack sat down on the edge of the bed and took her hand, rubbing it gently with his thumb. He said, "Okay, talk to me. What happened?"

"I think the cart accident made me remember something from *Mamm*'s death. Something I hadn't realized because we had been arguing when the horse raced ahead. But maybe it was just in the dream. Maybe it wasn't how things actually happened."

"Just tell me, Grace. Talking about it might jog your memory."

Grace sighed and bit her lower lip. What if she was wrong? She closed her eyes and thought of what she remembered of the dream. But she needed to go deeper than that. Taking a long breath and then letting it out, she heard the heart monitor slow down again, and allowed her mind to remember Amelia's death.

"It wasn't a car."

He gave her hand a squeeze. "Go on. What wasn't a car?"

"The horse didn't bolt because of a loud car. There had been a loud bang, but it wasn't a car. The horse took off running—no, *racing*. It started racing because it heard the starter gun." She opened her eyes. Having said the words spoken aloud made her realize how *ferhoodled* she was acting. "Never mind. That's impossible. It was just the distorted dream probably mixing up with the cart accident. Forget I said anything."

"I can't do that," Jack said. His face took on a serious expression. "What you're saying makes perfect sense."

"No, it doesn't. Nothing about that dream made sense. It was an accident because my *daed* purchased a bad horse."

"He purchased a good horse, but someone most likely switched his horse out for a top racer. Then someone else came to collect and thought shooting the gun would be the easiest way to do that. What happened to the horse after the accident?"

Grace sputtered at Jack's astronomical notions. "I was told he died. He was taken to the ranch's vet."

"By whom?"

"Hank, I think. I was too distraught to notice."

Jack nodded. "That would make sense. And someone would count on you being distracted."

"Are you saying they were stealing from my *daed* before they stole from me?"

"Yes."

Grace took a moment to let this realization sink in. "So, *Mamm*'s death wasn't caused by *Daed*'s poor horse purchase?"

"No."

The heart monitor picked up its pace. "Her death wasn't an accident." Tears pricked Grace's eyes.

"I'm sorry, Grace, but no, it was well planned."

"But why would they kill her if they only wanted the horse?"

"The only way to know that is to find our thief. And to find him before he kills again."

THIRTEEN

Early the next morning, Jack sat outside Grace's hospital room. He'd had a chair brought over for him during the night, but he hadn't dared sleep. He was glad, however, that she finally did. He hated seeing the deep sadness on her face after learning her mother's death most likely had not been an accident at all. As she'd restlessly slumbered, he'd spent the night putting connections together, making mental plans of his next steps to catch whoever was behind these crimes.

When Jack had arrived in Rogues Ridge, all he had was a case on stolen horses that had been sold into illegal horse racing. He had planned to come to Autumn Woods to figure out who the culprit was who'd stolen the horses, make an arrest, and be on his way. Never had he thought he would be dressed as an Amish man, protecting an Amish woman from someone who wanted her dead.

Jack lifted his shirt and reached past his gun for his cell phone, strapped to him under his clothes. He pressed the number for Nic and with the phone to his ear, waited for her to answer.

The phone rang four times before going to voice mail.

Jack checked the time on the clock at the end of the long hall. “6:30 a.m. She should be awake,” he mumbled in annoyance.

The elevator doors opened down the corridor just then, and out stepped Bishop Bontrager. He paused when he noticed Jack in his chair. Then he eyed the phone.

Jack cleared his throat and hit the end call button.

Bishop Bontrager slowly walked forward in silence until three feet separated them. Jack stood up and pocketed the phone as the elder asked, “Shall we talk?”

Jack could tell it wasn’t really a question, but an order. He faced the old man and nodded.

“I know you’re not related to the Millers. The sheriff came to me yesterday to share your past.”

Jack expected this. “Don’t you mean my record?”

“I will hold my judgment until I hear your side. But imagine my surprise when he told me your real name wasn’t Amos. Don’t lie to me again.”

Jack stood speechless for a moment. He was expecting the same reaction that he had received from his own bishop in Colorado. His community hadn’t even wanted to hear his reasons. His choices had disgraced them, and that was all they’d needed to cut him off.

As Jack decided how honest he would be with the elder, a nurse turned the corner at the end of the hall and walked toward them. He took in her features and filed them away without thought. He was a cop now and no longer an Amish man. His way of thinking no longer fitted into the peaceful and slow ways of the Amish. His mind had been trained for the darker side of life.

Once the nurse had passed them, Jack faced the bishop and said, "What you were told is true. Charges were dropped, but I did help a young woman out and transported a gun across state lines with her. That gun was then used to rob a convenience store, and I was framed for it. The law was understanding, but my family were not."

He waited for Bishop Bontrager to react, but seconds lapsed before the man sniffed and said, "Thank you for your honesty. Now, I have to ask why you are in Rogues Ridge."

Jack looked toward Grace's closed door. He knew the man was asking about his relationship with her, but that was not a topic he could discuss. He wasn't even sure he had an answer.

"I'm not getting in the way, if that's what you're thinking," Jack replied. "We come from different worlds."

Confusion crinkled the bishop's bushy eyebrows. "Are you saying you're not Amish?"

"I'm saying I have my views on certain topics that don't match hers." Jack breathed deeply through his nose. He thought of the gun under his shirt. If the cell phone had shocked the bishop, the gun would give him a heart attack.

"If you're speaking about her ideas of taking over for Benjamin as the horse trader, I understand your concern. It concerns us, as well. Hearing about her accident at the track has caused much distress within the community. It only proves she needs to see that our ways are for her protection."

Jack locked his gaze on Bishop Bontrager, sizing him up as quickly as he had the nurse. "Do you really care about her safety?"

The man sputtered. "What kind of question is that? I care for the safety of all my flock. That is why I have tried to convince her to marry."

"Leroy Mast."

Bishop Bontrager nodded firmly. "He's a *gut* man."

"That may be the case, but Grace needs to be the one to decide who's the right man for her." Jack's stomach twisted at the thought of Grace with anyone, but he tamped the feeling down before the bishop noticed his discomfort. Jack couldn't even explain his reaction… or the longing he had to be the man she chose.

Impossible.

"Grace is no longer at a marriageable age. Her choices are few."

"But they should still be her choices," Jack said. "All I'm saying is let her decide without pressure."

"As long as I know you aren't pressuring her, either."

Jack huffed. "She would never allow it."

Bishop Bontrager smirked. "No, I don't suppose she would. She is a strong-willed woman."

Jack studied the bishop with his bushy beard as white as snow and his kind, twinkling eyes. But could the man be trusted? Jack wanted to believe the bishop was innocent in all these crimes, but he couldn't risk it. Grace's life depended upon it. No one could be ruled out.

"It's too early for hospital visits, but can I trust you to tell her I stopped by?" Bishop Bontrager asked. "We are all worried about her. We want to see her back in the community again."

"I will."

He watched the bishop head down the hall and take the elevator down. After a few minutes, Jack took his chair and leaned back. At one end of the hall were the elevators, and he watched the numbers above the doors change, up and down. A few times the doors opened and hospital personnel came and went. Jack observed each one carefully. He doubted that the guy who'd come into Grace's room was going to attempt another visit. Still, he stayed on guard for the unexpected. As soon as he relaxed, the guy could strike.

The doors opened and two orderlies walked out with a wheelchair, chatting about a disgruntled boss. It sounded as though one of them was about to get fired. Jack studied his face.

A pimply twenty-year-old.

Blond hair.

Blue eyes.

Nearly six feet.

Not an ounce of muscle on him.

Loose scrubs that could hide a weapon.

The two men passed by, and the pimply faced kid nodded and said, "Good morning."

Jack noticed his high-top sneakers were untied. His gaze moved to the second orderly's shoes. His were covered with surgical booties, so Jack couldn't tell what kind he wore. He looked at his face and took note.

Long black hair pulled back in a ponytail. A paper mask covered his mouth. Jack estimated him to be between thirty and fifty. Being unable to see the orderly's face fully before he passed by made it impossible to say for sure.

At the end of the hall, they turned the corner and continued their complaining, until Jack couldn't hear them any longer.

The elevator doors opened again, and a nurse exited pushing a gurney. It was the one who'd passed Jack earlier, when he was with the bishop. Was she scoping the room?

The early morning staff must be starting to arrive as the sun rose. And Jack had yet to close his eyes. He took a deep breath and suppressed his exhaustion, for Grace's sake.

The nurse passed by again, but didn't greet him, her focus on her destination. She turned the corner and disappeared.

The intercom system beeped from the speaker above. "Paging all available doctors to the ER, stat," a concerned female voice said through the hallways. This early in the morning, the small hospital was no doubt working with a skeleton crew, and by the sound of the page, some sort of catastrophe was occurring downstairs.

Jack jumped to his feet, and his hand went to his gun. Something was off. He wondered if this was related to the search for Grace's attempted killer.

He walked to the end of the hall, itching to head down to the ER to find out. A set of doors opened just then and one of the orderlies appeared, returning with a gurney this time.

"What's going on in the ER?" Jack asked.

"Beats me," the guy said. It was the one with the ponytail, surgical mask and booties. "Probably some outraged family member not happy with the service." The guy laughed a bit to show he was joking.

Jack didn't return the laugh. "It sounds pretty serious." Like maybe the killer had hurt someone else.

Jack looked back at Grace's door. He really couldn't leave her. If anything happened to her, he would never forgive himself. He'd promised her he wouldn't leave her side.

The orderly turned the corner to head to the elevators, but as he did so the gurney tipped onto its side and clattered to the floor.

"Oh, man. That's never happened before," he said, bending to pick it up. "Thankfully, no one was on it. Could you imagine?"

Jack was glad to hear the guy had some sense. He went around to the bottom to help the orderly lift it. "Better be careful from now on. I'm sure that boss of yours wouldn't be too happy with you. You could be next to be fired."

The guy nodded and came to the end to take it from Jack. "I'd be canned, for sure. Thanks for the help."

In the next second, Jack felt a sharp pain in his thigh that had him gasping in confusion. A glance down showed a syringe sticking out of his leg. He looked back at the guy beside him. The surgical mask had slipped down a bit, exposing more of his face. Jack remembered seeing him somewhere, but before he could place him, his vision blurred and Jack fell forward on the gurney, the world going black.

First thing in the morning, Grace sat on the edge of her hospital bed while Dr. Reese fitted her with a brace.

"I know it's tight and restrictive, but your neck is too strained to hold up your head just yet."

"How long do I have to wear it?"

He shrugged. "As long as it takes. You'll know when it can come off when the pain subsides." He stepped back and assessed her vitals next. With a smile, he said, "I'm releasing you. I know it's soon, but I think your community is going to need your assistance."

"Why's that?"

Dr. Reese frowned. "I'm sorry to tell you this, but an Amish woman was brought into the ER early this morning with a GSW."

Grace squinted to show she didn't understand.

He explained further, "Sorry. A gunshot wound."

Grace inhaled so sharply her neck spasmed in pain. "How? Who?"

"I'm not sure. She was shot in the back. She was brought in unconscious and hasn't come to yet. Thankfully, your bishop was in the hospital."

"Bishop Bontrager is here? Right now?"

"He's in the waiting room downstairs. Once you're discharged you can head down to ICU and see for yourself." Reese checked her eyes with a light. "You still have a mild concussion, so take it easy. And absolutely no racing. Got it?"

"Not to worry about that, Doctor," a stern voice said from the doorway.

Dr. Reese turned, in the process clearing Grace's view of who had entered and interrupted.

"Leroy," she said, unsure why he was there. "How…?"

"How could I not know? The whole community

knows about your racing." He frowned and tossed his blond hair out of his eyes as he approached Dr. Reese's side. "I'll take her from here."

The doctor faced Grace with questioning eyes. "I'm sorry. I assumed the other Amish man was caring for you."

Leroy answered before Grace could say a word. "Not anymore. Bishop Bontrager has instructed me to come get her. She is our responsibility, and he has some things to discuss with her about her poor choices."

She looked pointedly at Leroy and said, "I have a job to do, and sometimes that means testing the horses out."

Leroy nodded. "We'll see what the bishop says about that. Right now, he's expecting you."

Grace swallowed hard, knowing she had gone too far with racing at the track. She could be in a lot of trouble. She squirmed, feeling a growing annoyance. But what could she say? Without her father to care for her, and her *mamm* dead, the bishop would step in to assign someone to fill that role.

And the whole community knew it would be Leroy.

"Are you all right with me releasing you to this man?" Dr. Reese asked.

Grace appreciated his concern, but there was no reason not to go with Leroy. And yet she shook her head and said, "I'd like to wait for Jack."

Leroy's eyes flared with anger. His lip curled, and Grace thought he would demand that she obey him. But in a flash, all expression of anger vanished. He smiled. "We can wait until he returns."

"Returns?" Grace squinted in confusion. "Isn't he right outside the room in his chair?"

"He wasn't there when I entered," Leroy said.

"Nor when I came, either," Dr. Reese confirmed. "I thought it strange he would leave you unprotected, knowing someone tried to hurt you."

Grace frowned, feeling disappointment, as well as a growing annoyance. She could have been killed. That idea frightened her, but she stood up from the bed and tempered her feelings. She was grateful for the collar, which assisted her in holding her head high. It gave her a semblance of dignity after having Jack let her down so carelessly.

Dr. Reese signed a piece of paper on a clipboard at the end of her bed and tore it off. Holding it out, he glanced from Grace to Leroy, then passed it to her. "You're free to go—when you think you're ready. Feel free to wait as long as you need. Would you like me to get an orderly to accompany you downstairs?"

Grace knew what he was really asking. *Do you feel safe, Grace?*

Without the ability to nod, the only way she could communicate was with her voice. She would have to state what she really wanted.

And that wasn't Leroy.

"*Ya*, I would like to have an orderly."

Dr. Reese went out to the hall and waved someone in. A moment later, a male with long black hair and wearing scrubs and a surgical mask low on his face entered the room with a wheelchair. Leroy stepped back for Grace to exit before him. As she passed he placed a hand on her shoulder. To the doctor, it may have looked like a gesture of comfort, but to Grace it felt like a walk to the woodshed.

She slowly settled her battered body into the conveyance, and as she was wheeled out, she took notice of the empty chair outside her door. It was where Jack had been keeping guard since she'd arrived the day before. Why had he left her side? She felt as though one of her horses had kicked her in the gut.

"Did you see where the Amish man who sat here went?" she asked the orderly as they moved past. The frantic beat of her heart had her gripping the arms of the wheelchair. She needed Jack to know where she was being taken.

"I haven't seen another Amish man," the orderly said from behind her as he whisked her toward the elevators.

Leroy stepped up to her side. "We both know that man is not Amish. It's time to stop lying and come clean. Who is he and why is he living at your home? And now that other woman, who is also not Amish…? I wish you had come to me, Grace. She could die, and this will hurt our community."

Grace tried to turn her head, but couldn't. "What do you mean, die? What happened to Nic?" Her voice shook, then fear set in. "Where's *Daed*?"

"She was shot, and I have no idea where Benjamin is. Bishop Bontrager sent me out there, but the place was empty."

"They got him," Grace cried, and started to stand.

A hand covered her shoulder. "You have to stay seated, ma'am," the orderly told her. "It's the hospital's requirement until I get you to the door."

"But my father could be hurt somewhere. Jack needs to find him."

"Who is Jack?" Leroy asked, his voice growing impatient. "Do you mean Amos? Is Jack his real name? Tell me the truth, Grace. Once and for all. What have you gotten into? No more lying."

Grace didn't like to be accused of lying, and Jack had told her if she was ever asked who he was, she was to tell the truth.

The orderly pushed her up to the elevator and came around the front of the chair to press the button. With the neck brace fastened in place, Grace could only look straight at the man's back, where his long black ponytail dangled. She dropped her gaze to his booties over his shoes.

The doors opened, and he returned to his place behind her. She tried to see his face, but without the ability to turn her head, she barely caught a glimpse. He pushed her in, so she was facing the back wall. She heard the doors close behind her, and the next second, she heard a thud.

"Is something wrong?" Grace asked, trying to turn her body to see behind her. A hand touched her shoulder again and held her in place.

"Everything's fine." The voice was a gentle whisper and she assumed Leroy had once again calmed himself.

Grace sighed and decided she would be honest with Leroy. She really had no other choice. "We had a valid reason for hiding his identity, Leroy. He's an FBI agent here to investigate a crime. I need you to keep this secret, or these criminals will get away with what they've done." Grace felt her lips tremble, and she closed her eyes, thinking of what else she needed him to know. "My *mamm*'s death wasn't an accident. Someone caused her apparent 'accident.'" Someone killed her, Leroy. And they tried to kill me. And now they have my *daed*."

Grace held her breath as she waited for Leroy's reaction. His silence spoke volumes. He had to be in shock at all she had just told him.

"I know it's a lot to understand. We try to live a simple life separate from the English, but sometimes our worlds do overlap, and not always in the best ways. But can I trust you not to say anything just yet? Until we know who's behind the crimes, the FBI needs to do their job. We can't interrupt that."

Still, silence loomed.

"Leroy?" Grace tried to turn, but the hand settled on her shoulder again.

Grace didn't receive a reply, only a sharp pain in her arm. She couldn't turn her head to see what had jabbed her, but she let out a weak scream before sleep crept over her. *Some sort of drug,* she thought in her muddled state. She also knew she'd just given Jack's identity away to the bad guy—who probably had already gotten to him.

"Jack never would have left my side," she mumbled. "Where is he..." She didn't finish her sentence as darkness descended.

FOURTEEN

Jack opened his eyes and inhaled deeply. Pitch-black darkness surrounded him, and a powerful cold seeped into his bones.

Stay calm.

He slowed his panicked breaths to allow his mind to figure out where he was. He was lying flat, with his arms by his sides. He tried to move them, but hit something hard on both sides, and as he slowly raised them, touched more cold metal.

"Help!" he yelled, but didn't want to use up any remaining oxygen, so waited to see if someone came to his aid.

When there was no reply, he felt his body to see if his hidden gun and phone were still strapped to him under his clothes. Finding those items, he breathed a bit easier. Whoever had stuffed him in here didn't think to pat him down. They really believed he was Amish, and that was good for Grace. She would be safer if the perp didn't know the FBI was onto him.

Jack pulled up his shirt and retrieved his phone. Switching it on brought the screen to full brightness.

Lifting it, he saw the ceiling was less than a foot away from his face. Turning the device, he looked to his right and left. He was enclosed in a metal box. The smell told him where it was located. With that putrefactive odor, he could be in only one place.

The morgue.

That orderly who obviously was not part of the medical staff had stuffed him in a drawer down here in the hospital's basement. But for how long?

Jack tried to call Nic, but the closed metal drawer didn't allow phone reception. He was also almost out of battery power, which told him he'd been down here for many hours. He had to get to Grace before this guy did. But dropping his head back, Jack figured he was too late. The thug wouldn't have wasted a moment to get to her.

Jack did the only thing he could: he raised his arms above his head and started banging on the frigid metal above him. Someone was bound to hear him and come to his aid.

"Is someone out there?" he yelled. "Help!"

Over and over he called out, with no response. Twisting as best he could in the confined space, Jack felt the edges of the door, checking for any hinges or latches. It seemed everything was on the outside.

In frustration, he banged his fist on it one more time, just as the door flew wide and revealed a terrified-looking woman on the other side.

She opened her mouth to let loose a scream, and Jack held up his hands to try to calm her fear.

"I know what this looks like, but I wasn't dead. I'm FBI. Someone shoved me in here. Please pull me out."

The frightened woman shrank back, shaking her head.

"Please, someone's life depends on me getting to her in time. Just pull open this thing, and I'll be on my way."

The woman took a tentative step forward, gingerly grabbed the drawer he was in and pulled it out.

Jack jumped out and ran for the door. "Thank you! I hope this doesn't scar you for life." He was running down the hall to the elevator before he realized she'd opened the morgue door to watch him go. The elevator opened and he stepped in. As he pressed the button for Grace's floor, he waved to the woman, who was shaking her head as the doors closed.

When the elevator reached Grace's floor, Jack bolted out and ran into Dr. Reese.

"There you are," the doctor said. "I was hoping to see you. I just released Grace to the other Amish man. It made me uneasy without you there."

Jack nearly grabbed the lapels of Reese's white coat. "What do you mean, you released her?"

"I made sure to ask her if she was ready to go. She agreed she was content, going with Leroy."

"Leroy Mast took her?" Jack tried to wrap his mind around this information. He hit the button for the elevator repeatedly, but the door wouldn't open, so he started racing for the stairwell.

"Wait!" Dr. Reese called. "They're downstairs in ICU. One of their own has been shot."

Jack halted at the news, just as the elevator dinged and the doors finally opened.

Dr. Reese's face drained of all color. "Nurse!" he yelled. "I need assistance!"

Jack ran back into the hall and approached the elevator. The doctor was hunched over someone sprawled on the floor inside. The simple black pants that matched Jack's own told him they belonged to an Amish man.

But who?

Dr. Reese glanced back at Jack as a team of medical personnel ran from the workstation with a wheelchair. "It's Leroy. I don't understand. He left with the orderly who wheeled her out."

Dr. Reese might not understand, but Jack did. "That was not an orderly. That was a killer."

Grace sat in an upholstered chair in the most luxurious room she'd ever seen. It was fancier than her imagination could concoct, with its velvety curtains and a carpet so thick she was tempted to take her boots off and sink her toes into it. Her feet had healed enough to feel the lush pile. The small ornate table in front of her would have been frowned upon by the Amish, with their simple and sturdy furniture designs, but Grace doubted any Amish furniture would suffice in this elegant room.

She reached out for the delicate china plate on the table and ran her finger around the gold edging. She wondered if was real and thought about the price of something so fine. Another thing she couldn't fathom. As well as the gold fork beside the plate.

She picked it up and tested its weight, then turned it so that it was shielded in her palm. It might make for a potential weapon.

Guilt swamped her at the thought, but until she knew why she'd woken up in this place and who had brought her here after knocking her out, she felt like a little protection was called for. Jack would be proud of her, but she hated that she'd been put in this situation.

All she remembered was leaving the hospital room with Leroy, but how would Leroy know about this place? Was there more to him than she ever knew? Did he have a dark, evil side?

Across the small parlor a fire crackled in the fireplace, with a large chair positioned in front of it. It beckoned to her. Still in her neck brace, she stood carefully to walk over to it. But when she reached it, she saw three framed photographs on the mantel and bypassed the chair for a closer look.

Grace picked up one picture frame and gazed at a family of four staring back at her, a couple with two young children.

Being Amish, Grace never had pictures taken of herself. No graven images were allowed, but she had seen a few photographs of English people. Their still images were a moment frozen in time. Grace wondered who these people were and when it had been taken. Were these children still young? Or had they grown up since this picture was snapped?

She looked to the next photograph and believed she had her answer. Especially when it appeared the two children were teenagers in it. Grace looked first at the boy and remembered seeing him before.

It was a younger version of the man in the sports car who had stopped to yell at her and Jack the first day they came to the track.

Was that where she was? Was she in the house at Autumn Woods?

She looked around the room and thought it might belong in such a house. But the room had no windows, so there was no way to look out and see the ranch and track. There was one door in the corner that she'd already tried and found it locked. There was no way of escaping. Nothing to do but wait. But for what? Death?

Grace forced the thought from her mind and returned her attention back to the picture in her hand. She looked at the teenage girl to the left of the boy. She also looked familiar, but Grace wasn't sure how she knew her.

In the next second, recognition hit Grace as hard as the ground had the day of the horse trial accident.

Slowly, Grace stepped back, in complete shock at who she was seeing. The back of her legs hit the chair, and she fell into it, clutching the frame in a tight grip.

"*Mamm*," Grace said in a whisper. The girl in the photograph was a younger version of her mother, and an English one.

Grace always knew Amelia had once been English, even though they hadn't spoken of it much. But she'd never thought of her mother looking any different from how Grace knew her.

As an Amish woman.

But Amelia Miller had once been a completely different person. She'd worn jewelry and makeup. Her clothes were fancy, and she'd smiled in pictures.

Grace looked around at the expensive room and realized her *mamm* also had money. She'd come from a wealthy home and gave it all up to become Amish and marry the man she loved.

Grace figured her *mamm* must have met Benjamin

when he came to bid on the horses. They fell in love and she broke off ties with her family forever. Because she left, her father cut her off, never speaking to her again.

Had Amelia ever regretted leaving her family? She'd never let on if she did.

Grace studied her photo and took in her smile. It was pretty enough, but Grace remembered the joy in her mother's eyes that this picture did not capture. Grace had to believe her *mamm* had been content with her decision and wouldn't have changed a thing.

But perhaps someone here didn't feel the same way.

Was that why she'd been brought here? Did someone want her to know the truth about her mother?

A locked clicked, and the doorknob turned, capturing Grace's full attention. She rose to her feet, with the frame in one hand and the fork clutched tightly in the palm of the other.

She was about to find out the truth, but there was a chance she would have to fight for it.

The one thing she didn't want to do.

FIFTEEN

Jack burst from the hospital's main entrance with his phone in his hand. He'd called Nic twice now, with no answer, and couldn't help but think something was wrong on her end, as well. With the phone to his ear, he scanned the parking lot for some sort of ride while he called again.

"Come on, pick up, Nic," he said in frustration, and groaned when it went to voice mail again.

With no one in the parking lot, Jack ran out onto the street of downtown Rogues Ridge.

That's when he saw the horse and buggy tethered to a hitching post.

Turning back around, he faced the small hospital and remembered what Dr. Reese had said. An Amish person had been shot.

Jack looked at his phone with the unfathomable at the forefront of his mind. He pressed his hand to the top of his head.

"No," he said aloud, taking the first steps back toward the building. The emergency room entrance was off to the side, and he headed in that direction, his feet picking up in speed as he neared the sliding doors. Dr. Reese wouldn't know Nic wasn't really Amish. He wouldn't know the clothes were only a cover and would think she was one of the community members.

But no one would come to help her.

Jack needed to find Grace, but he couldn't leave without learning the status of his supervisor. Especially if she could die because she had come to his aid.

He pushed through the entrance and ran past the front desk for the ICU doors at the end of the hall. After a few painful minutes of waiting, the doors opened, and a nurse stepped out. Jack skirted past her and grabbed a door before it shut and locked on him. Slipping inside, he pulled the door closed and faced a corridor of glassed-in rooms.

Another nurse stepped out of a room to his right. When she caught sight of him, she approached him and whispered, "You shouldn't be in here."

"I know, but I need to know about the Amish woman who was shot. She was brought in this morning." The last part was probably unnecessary. How many Amish women had come into this hospital lately with a GSW? Or ever?

The nurse eyed the room she'd just exited then looked back at Jack. "She's out of surgery, but she has not regained consciousness. Would you like to see her? I can allow two in."

"Two?" Jack looked around, but he stood alone. "It's just me."

"There's another man with her now. The bishop, I believe."

Jack stared at the glass walls as his mind raced with

reasons Thomas Bontrager would be with Nic. "I'd like to see her, thank you." He headed that way and found the white-haired elder sitting by her side.

Jack entered on quiet footsteps, his gaze zeroing in on the pale, sleeping face of his boss in the bed. She didn't look alive, even though the machines said otherwise. An oxygen mask covered her nose and mouth, and life-saving air puffed into her lungs.

"Who is she?" Bishop Bontrager asked quietly, as Jack came up alongside the bed. "The hospital staff want to know, but I don't have an answer for them. She must have family who should be here."

Jack's chest tightened as he realized he didn't know much about her family. She seldom spoke about them. "I think she has a father in New Mexico," he said, drawing on a few conversations they'd had. "She works so much. The job is really her life."

"And what job is that?" The elder angled a pointed stare his way. "The truth. I deserve that after having found her in a pool of her own blood."

"You found her?" Jack asked. "What about Benjamin?" He looked back at the open door. "Did you bring him?"

"Benjamin was nowhere around."

The world closed in on Jack, squeezing the air from his own lungs to the point he might need a respirator, too. "So he's got them both," he muttered, admitting his failure aloud. "I messed up again." His knees threatened to buckle and bring him down.

Bishop Bontrager pursed his lips. "I'm still waiting for an answer."

"She's not Amish. And neither am I," Jack stated

abruptly. “She’s my boss. We’re FBI. I left my Amish community eight years ago and became a cop. I now work as an agent for Nic. Her name is Nicole Harrington, and she gave me a case to work on. I came to Rogues Ridge to investigate a horse theft ring at Autumn Woods that led me to the Millers. I know now they were being set up to take the fall, but things have gone from thefts to attempted murder, and I need your help.”

The bishop’s eyes squinted, and he looked at Nic’s still form.

“Did you hear me? Grace and Benjamin are missing. I was told Leroy Mast took Grace from the hospital this morning, but his unconscious body was just found in the elevator.”

The bishop turned to Jack, his impassive face and still body the picture of a calm leader. “An officer will be here at any minute. Deputy Cassie Shaw answered my call and helped phone the ambulance to bring… Nic in,” he explained. “Deputy Shaw will be back in a moment, and you can talk to her. I think it’s time to get the local law enforcement involved, don’t you?”

Jack frowned, but nodded. “I waited too long as it is.”

“So while we wait, please sit.” Bishop Bontrager invited Jack to the second chair in the small room. “I want you to finish your story about yourself. I’m stunned that we’ve had an ex-Amish Englisher in our midst this whole time. Looking at you, I would’ve never guessed it.”

“I do a lot of undercover work,” Jack said, and glanced out the wall of glass, willing the officer to arrive quickly. With a sigh, he did as the bishop asked and took the chair, sitting on the edge, ready to jump back up. "You're not supposed to guess that I'm a fake. To do so would put my safety at risk."

Jack looked at Nic and realized how her safety had been forfeited. "My boss may lose her life, and Grace and Benjamin may lose theirs if I don't find them."

"Marder," the bishop said to himself. He spoke of murder as calmly as one does the weather. His hands were folded in his lap as though he had been praying. "I have a confession to make, and I hope you can forgive me."

Jack sat motionless on the edge of his seat, stunned that this bishop would ask him for forgiveness. "I told you I'm not Amish anymore. Why would you want my forgiveness?"

"Your head may say you're not Amish, but your heart says otherwise."

"I once led with my heart, and that got me into trouble." Jack thought of the girl who'd needed protection from an abusive boyfriend. "*Ya*, I didn't think it through. I should have used my head. I met a girl on the run, and instead of going to the police, she wanted her father's gun brought to her. I knew in my head it was wrong, but I did it anyway, leaving my prints all over that gun. Her abusive boyfriend got ahold of it and used it to rob a convenience store. He dressed like an Amish boy, and before I knew it, I was accused of the crime. The charges were soon dropped when the truth came out, but my community was a whole other trial and jury. To them, I had lost my way."

"Well, I don't think so," Bishop Bontrager said. He

sighed deeply. "Don't ever regret following your heart, Jack. But if you do find yourself far off track, face your mistake head on and make amends. You can't finish the race set before you by *Gött* if you avoid your mistakes. Throw off that baggage and keep moving forward. Which is why I need to ask for forgiveness. I, too, lost my way for a little while. I let my own wants get in the way of what my heart was telling me. So, before it goes so far that I can't find my way back, I want to rectify this now. I am sorry I came between you and Grace."

"What?" Jack questioned what he'd heard. "Grace and I could never be."

"That's your head talking again. Start listening to your heart, before you lose what's important to you again."

The double doors opened in the hall. They both glanced out the glass wall.

"It looks like the sheriff is here," Bishop Bontrager said.

A few seconds later Sheriff Maddox and a woman deputy stepped through into the hallway. They wore their official business expressions, and Jack had never thought he would be glad to see the man.

"Before they get in here, I need to know, can you forgive me?" Bishop Bontrager asked Jack. "I will no longer push Grace into a marriage with Leroy. I will let her heart, also, decide."

"Of course. But the main question is will you be able to forgive me if Grace and Benjamin can't be found?" With that, Jack stood to go out and meet the sheriff and deputy. Time was wasting, and every second that went by was one second closer to losing Grace forever.

Jack fought a wave of pain at the thought. It made his stomach roil and tears fill his eyes. He pressed his palms to his eyelids, then stepped up to the two lawmen, ready to turn over the reins and ask for help. Anything to save Grace.

"I need to speak to you out in the waiting room," he said and led the way to a private room for family. Thankfully it was empty, and he didn't waste another second. "Grace is missing. Actually, she was kidnapped from the hospital," he told them, then explained who Nic was and who he really was, and how an orderly had drugged him and taken Grace.

Hank sent Jack a heated stare after the explanation was finished. His jaw ticked. "FBI, you say. This is my jurisdiction. I don't like not knowing when an investigation is going on under my nose. You could have alerted me."

"I couldn't risk it. I was undercover, and to blow it could have put other people in danger. Please, we don't have time. We can hash this out later. My boss was already shot. Do you know where Benjamin is?"

The sheriff looked at him, obviously contemplating whether to believe him. Then he said, "Benjamin was nowhere on the property. Believe me, I looked. I still have my guys searching." Hank squinted and asked, "But you say an orderly took Grace? Did you get a good look at this guy?"

"I only saw the one who drugged me. He had black hair, long and pulled back in a ponytail. Blue eyes, and he was in good shape, but still middle-aged, maybe."

Jack left off the part about the man having to lift him after he'd knocked Jack out with whatever was in that syringe. That couldn't have been an easy task.

"Clothes?"

"He was in scrubs. His shoes were in surgical booties."

Hank scoffed and waved at the nurses' station ahead. "Great, that could be anyone here."

"I'm pretty sure it's someone at Autumn Woods. I know I've seen the face before. I believe it was there. A stable hand, maybe. I want to go search the place. I'd like your assistance to gain access."

"Oh, now I'm supposed to help you, after you kept me in the dark?"

"Please, Sheriff," Bishop Bontrager interjected from the opened door. "These are my flock. I would hate to have something horrible happen to them."

Hank paused but nodded once to show he understood. He turned to Jack. "Okay, you can come in my cruiser, but don't mess with my equipment. I like my things in a particular order. And I do things my way. Got it?"

"Got it."

"Good. Deputy Shaw, stay behind in case the FBI agent wakes up. I want to know as soon as she does." Hank leered at Jack. "I have a complaint against one of her men."

Jack would let the man make as many complaints as he wanted, just as long as he helped him bring Grace and Benjamin home alive.

SIXTEEN

Grace braced herself at the sound of the doorknob turning. Someone was about to enter her elegant room of confinement. Slowly the door swung wide and revealed a cart with two covered plates, napkins and a single bloodred rose in a vase. Grace raised her gaze from the cart to the person wheeling it and shrank back.

"Liam?" she said. Her mind stalled as she attempted to process why the stable hand was delivering her a food cart. "What's happening? Why am I here?"

The young man barely looked at her as he pushed the cart inside and focused on unloading the two meals.

"Are you staying to eat?" she asked and walked around the table to force him to face her. "Please answer me. What is going on? Why have I been kidnapped?"

His head shot up, and he shook it once as he eyed her neck brace and frowned. "This wasn't supposed to happen." He threw a glance at the opened door and busied himself with preparing the table.

"I'm not going to eat, so you might as well take this all away," she informed him, but he took the covers off both plates and put them on the cart. Next, he backed the cart out into the hall and turned to shut the door.

Grace ran as fast as her injured body would let her to try and stop it from closing, and to make him tell her why she was there. "Don't go. I need to know. Please."

His face a mask of worry, Liam nodded at the table. "You'll find out soon." With that he pulled the door closed.

Grace walked the last few steps and placed her palm on the door. She leaned in, laid her head awkwardly against her hand and closed her eyes as tears welled up in them. She prayed for the strength to face whatever was coming her way. Whatever she was going to find out. God would never allow something to happen that He hadn't determined to be His will. He would take this horrifying situation and turn it for *gut*. Grace had to believe in His promises...but she also wouldn't be putting down the fork.

Her *daed* would frown at her for taking up a weapon. It wasn't the Amish way, to fight, but it wasn't too often Amish persons found themselves kidnapped, either. "Your will be done, Lord, but if that means You want me to fight back, I pray You will guide me and show me."

And help Daed to understand and forgive me if I do.

She thought of Jack and how his family hadn't offered him forgiveness when he did something he thought was right. It was so hard to know sometimes, in the heat of the moment, what the right thing was. *Maybe if I escape, I can avoid it altogether.*

Grace reached for the doorknob, but as she knew it would be, found it locked. She turned her body to gaze about the room. Without any windows, it must be in the basement, she believed—the fanciest basement she'd ever seen, but then it was a fancy house.

Grace put her hand on the wall behind her and made her way around the room, feeling for any sign of another exit. Every surface felt solid and impenetrable. She was about halfway around when the lock clicked again, and Grace dropped her hand to face the door, the fork in her palm and at the ready.

The door opened in and an older version of the man in the photograph stood in the doorway. He was also the man who yelled at her that day behind the stables. "Hello, Grace. We meet again," he said with a slight smile. "Edmund Barone, in case you don't remember." He walked to the small table laden with the two full plates. "Please, join me. We have much to discuss."

Grace didn't move. "I'm not hungry. I just want to know why I'm here. Are you going to let me go?"

The man frowned. Then he pulled out a chair for her. "We will eat and talk. It's been a long day, and I *am* hungry. Please, come sit. My cook made a lovely meal for you. She was happy to prepare it for you."

"Me?" Grace pointed to herself. "How does she know me?"

"She doesn't, but she knew your mother."

Grace glanced to the photograph she'd left on the chair, then quickly back at the man. "I see you did, too," she said warily.

He nodded. "Amelia was my sister." He gestured around the room. "And this was her home."

Grace swallowed hard. "I gathered that, but why am *I* here?"

"I thought it was time to formally meet my niece. When Amelia left to become Amish, our father made it known she was dead to us. Then I recently heard she really did die, and I was in shock. I guess in the back of my mind, I thought I had lots of time to make amends. But I was wrong. I was too late with my father, and I was too late with her." He sighed, then lifted his chin. "Then I saw you back behind the barn. When you told me that your father was the horse trader for the Amish, I knew instantly who you were. You were Amelia's daughter, and I had a second chance to make amends."

"By kidnapping me? And hurting Leroy?"

"The men will be fine. I used a tranquilizer that we have for the horses. I'm sure they're awake already, even if the other guy is locked up tight." He smirked. "The little one is probably already home on the farm, but the big guy might have some nightmares after he wakes up and realizes he's sleeping with the dead."

"Big guy? Dead?" Grace asked in confusion. Then it became clear. "Do you mean Jack?" She stormed forward, her fork drawn and pointed at this man who was supposedly her *onkel*. "What did you do to him?"

Edmund didn't flinch. Not one eyelash twitched at her violent demand. He didn't even look at the fork, but only at her.

Heavy silence filled the room, then his nostrils flared before he said, "Sit."

A sinking feeling filled Grace as she realized she had no choice but to follow orders. Her chest tightened at the thought of Jack being harmed. And what did this monster mean when he said Jack was sleeping with the dead?

She approached the chair and slowly sat down. "Please tell me he will be all right."

Edmund sat in the other chair and lifted his napkin, spreading it across his lap. "I see you have feelings for him. This surprises me. Perhaps you would have come here willingly, after all."

Grace barely heard anything after the word *feelings*. He thought she had feelings for Jack? "Why would you say such a thing?"

"I didn't think you would agree to come to an Englisher's home, but knowing that your Jack is actually English, I guess I was wrong. If you like him, maybe you would have."

"How do you know Jack is an Englisher?" she asked.

"You told me at the hospital. I was pretending to be the orderly."

"You had black hair."

"A wig. Just like your Jack."

So he knew. She had thought she was telling Leroy that Jack was an FBI agent, but really, she had been telling this man while he was kidnapping her. She'd given away Jack's cover. "Why did you lock him up?"

"I needed some extra time."

"For what?"

"To offer you a new home."

"I don't understand. I have a home. With my *daed*."

"But you could have all this. You could be your own boss. Not just your own, but the only boss. You could care for the horses. You could buy your own racers, the best of the breeds. This could all be yours, just as it was supposed to be Amelia's."

Grace felt like she was back on the racing cart again,

careening around corners at a breakneck speed. Every word Edmund said to her blurred by her in confusion. "You kidnapped me to give me a house?" Her voice squeaked at the absurdity of such a thing.

"Would you have come otherwise?"

"No." She answered without a thought, because the question didn't need any thinking on.

"Then I would do it again." He picked up his fork and jabbed a tomato in his salad. "This is what you do with a fork, by the way." He raised it to his mouth and started chewing slowly. "And before you discredit my offer, consider what a life as an Englisher could mean. You could have a relationship with your Jack. Just think about it."

"What you're saying is impossible. It would never be allowed. I'm Amish."

"And Amelia was English before she chose to become Amish. She fell in love with the Amish horse trader's son and married him. Anything's possible." Edmund shrugged. "Let's eat. We'll talk about how we can make this work after the meal."

Grace breathed deeply and followed his command, but no matter how much she chewed, she thought for sure she would choke. Her throat swelled and wanted to reject anything she put into her mouth. Eating was not what she wanted right now.

She wanted answers.

She wanted to know if her father was safe.

And she wanted Jack.

Her stomach clenched at the thought. She couldn't justify such a feeling. It was forbidden, but Edmund's temptation hung in front of her and made her question the possibility.

Grace shook her head, clearing away the idea and the vision it created in her mind. "No."

"No what? No to Jack, or no to all this?"

"No to both." Grace stood up. She wished she could look down on this man, but her brace wouldn't allow it. It was just as well, because it would have been wrong to show such anger.

She took a deep breath and said, "There's a reason *Mamm* left here and never looked back, and it didn't have anything to do with your father not allowing any contact. She loved being Amish, and she loved my *daed.* And I have to think of what she would want me to do if she were here, and that is to leave and never come back."

Edmund placed his fork down and folded his arms in front of him on the table. A smile played on his lips. "You sound just like Amelia. Man, I miss her." The smile flitted away. "I'm sorry things have come to this. It's not how it was supposed to be, but have it your way. I will also have mine."

Liam's words came back to Grace. *"This wasn't supposed to happen."* But what did those cryptic words mean?

"How are things supposed to be?" she dared to ask.

Edmund pursed his lips. "Well, first, my father should have left me this place. It was supposed to be me running the ranch, but instead he decided to snub me one last time and leave it to my sister." A darkness filtered into his eyes as they stared straight at Grace. "The very sister who turned her back on us and our way of life for a farmhouse and cornfields. For some reason, Father thought she would make a better heir."

"*Mamm* inherited all of this? D-did she know?" Grace could barely process the information. "She couldn't have known."

"She did. And she made the same mistake you're making right now. She closed the door in the attorney's face when he went to tell her. She closed the door on me."

Grace's throat closed at the snarled warning threading through Edmund's voice. "We just want to live peacefully," she explained.

He laughed in a sickly way and raised his hands. "And that's all I want, too. But I can't live out my days here. Not without your help."

"Why me?"

"Because you're Amelia's next of kin. You now own this place and everything on the property."

Dead silence hung in the room. Grace tried to swallow, but it felt like her neck brace tightened, preventing any air from passing. "Everything?" Her voice squeaked as she spoke, gazing down at her gold plate.

Edmund smirked. "Don't get too excited. What you see in this room is the last of dear old Dad's belongings worth anything. I've slowly been making things disappear since he died. I came home thinking it would all be mine. When I found out he made sure none of it would, I decided to take it all another way."

Grace jumped to her feet, sending the chair backward to the floor, but it barely made a sound on the plush carpet. "The horses," she blurted. The thefts became clear. "You've been stealing the thoroughbreds, and you've been framing my father for them. And me. You used us to swap out the horses for the ones we bought, then arranged to steal them from our barn later. Then you sold them illegally and took the money."

Grace stepped away from the table, but stopped when she realized she couldn't go anywhere. She was held captive by this manipulative thief. "It's no wonder my mother left this place behind forever. Did you—" Grace halted abruptly, not asking the question that needed answering. Could she handle the truth?

"Did I kill her?" Edmund frowned.

Grace nodded.

"It was meant to be a warning to her to comply with my wishes. Her death was unfortunate, an accident, really. I'm not a killer. I only wanted her help and she refused."

"Like you want mine now." Grace's voice dulled as this man's twisted version of the truth came out. Whether or not Edmund Barone admitted his evil doings, he was a killer. Amelia Miller was dead because of him and his need for money. "You killed my mother."

"You won't ever prove any such thing. I wasn't even there," he said smugly, and took another bite of his salad as though he was discussing the weather.

Frustration had Grace clenching her fists at her sides. "Did you try to kill me, too?"

"You mean the horse trial accident? You weren't meant to be racing that day." He pointed to his neck. "Sorry you had to experience such a terror."

Grace touched her brace as his words sank in. "Steven Byler was supposed to be racing Game Changer. What had he done?"

Edmund's lip curled. "He put his nose where it didn't belong and notified the FBI. Your big guy came calling. If I had known at the hospital who he was I would have made sure he really belonged in the morgue."

Morgue? Nausea rolled through Grace. She needed to get out of here fast, to get to Jack. She needed Sheriff Maddox. He would know what to do. But for now, she had to figure a way out.

"What do you want from me?" she asked.

Edmund leaned back in his chair, and a slow smile spread across his face. "Maybe you're smarter than your mother, after all." He clapped his hands and stood up. "To the stable we go. You're going to help me steal Game Changer."

Grace scoffed. "People will notice her missing."

"I'm burning the place to the ground. By the time they figure it out, I'll be long gone. And unless you want to be, too, you'll follow my orders."

Edmund grabbed hold of Grace's upper arm and led her down a hall and up a flight of stairs. If she thought the room she'd been in was ornate and fancy, she hadn't seen anything yet. Though she feared what Edmund had planned for her, she couldn't help but be awed by the splendor of the home. Most of the rooms he pushed her past were empty, but still, the house was magnificent. The idea that her *mamm*, who'd lived the perfect Amish life, came from such grandeur stupefied Grace at every turn. By the time they'd made it to the front hall, Grace questioned if she'd ever really known Amelia Miller.

Or Amelia Barone.

She stood in the center of a large empty room with

a ceiling as high as her barn and gazed up at a glowing chandelier that hinted at a lifestyle not of this world.

"Don't get too attached to the place," Edmund said. "It won't be yours for much longer."

Grace dismissed his words. "I can't be tempted by such worldly things. The plain life is all I want."

"Then why aren't you married? Most Amish I've heard of are married with children by the time they're your age."

Grace couldn't discredit his observation. "I was needed at home. My *daed* needed my help with the horse trading. Do you have him? Is he safe? He's all I care about. He needs me."

Edmund studied her for a moment, then said, "I think I see now. You chose to put your life on hold to help your mentally ailing father do his job." He opened the front door of the mansion and allowed her to view the sweeping landscape of Autumn Woods from high on the hill. Evening had arrived in this horrible day, but the day wasn't over yet. "And now you're going to help me."

Grace inhaled sharply as he yanked her through the door. They stepped out onto a huge stone patio with large planters and a gabled covering. Comfortable furnishings beckoned passersby to sit for a while, but all Grace could think was how it was just a facade.

"It is a beautiful place," Edmund said as he watched her. "I often wondered how Amelia could give it up. I contacted her once, about two years into her marriage, and asked her if she was ready to return to the good life."

"Good life?" The term made Grace cringe.

Edmund laughed at her expression. "That's the same look she gave me. She said she had chosen the good life, and Benjamin was her home now. Still, I think she struggled for a long time. She didn't have you for years."

Grace contemplated that as he practically dragged her down the long winding drive. She'd often wondered why her parents didn't have her for nearly ten years after they married. She'd always assumed it wasn't by choice, but perhaps her *mamm* had needed the time to accustom herself to her new way of life.

Her *gut* life.

Grace smiled, knowing Amelia had chosen a wonderful life for herself, but also for her child.

They walked the rest of the way in silence, until they reached the back of the stable, where they'd first met. Edmund opened the door and held it for her to enter before him.

She stepped inside, instantly met by the familiar sweet smell of the horses' home. She heard the nicker and huff of one that detected their presence. A crunch of hay said the animal was moving up to meet them. Grace approached the stall and gave the horse her hand to nibble on.

"I don't have anything for you, sorry," she murmured, rubbing its head before stepping back.

"How many horses have you stolen?" Grace asked, without looking Edmund's way. She wondered if he would be honest with her.

His chest puffed with pride, and he smiled smugly. "I've moved seven horses without the estate even realizing it. That was, until Steven alerted the FBI." His smile turned menacing.

"So who was switching them with the horses we bid on?" Grace asked.

"Liam has been eager to help. Money talks."

"*He* was the one who came to collect the thoroughbred at my home and shot at me?"

"He shot at your agent. Never at you. That was my stipulation. I needed you alive to help me right my father's wrong." Edmund moved down to the third stall, where the placard read Game Changer. His smile was back. "The prize of the whole stable."

Grace couldn't fathom this man's selfishness. "You could have killed her in that racing accident."

"Nah, I made sure she could run off unscathed," Edmund said.

He opened the stall door and led the horse out. She bobbed her head at Grace and nickered.

Grace reached up and hugged her, pressing her face into the thoroughbred's neck and scrunching her mane with her fingers. Game Changer really was a prize.

But she wasn't the real prize.

Getting out of here alive would be. And Grace needed to do it quickly before she became the victim of another so-called accident.

Edmund went about saddling the horse. "You'll ride her out. It won't be long before she throws you. I had to get her used to the cart so I could pull off Steven's accident that you took his place for."

"The Amish don't ride horses," she tried to delay with a reason his idea wouldn't work. "It would be highly suspect."

"You're a horse thief. I don't think this infraction will really matter." He dropped a step stool beside Game Changer. "Climb up. Now."

Grace tried to breathe deeply, but barely filled her lungs. Once on Game Changer, she knew she was being sent on a wild chase she most likely would not survive. A glance back at Edmund showed him holding a long leather riding crop. He flicked it and the snap made Game Changer's coat ripple when she twitched at the sound. The animal was ready to race.

"Why did you try to smother me at the hospital if you needed me to steal this horse?"

"Smother you? What are you talking about?" Edmund squinted up at her. "I never..." He glanced at the stable's closed double doors. In the next second, he reached up and dragged her off the horse, then grasped Grace's wrist and entwined the leather strap around it. "Change of plans for now. Back to the house."

"Why?"

"Seems I have a traitor in my midst, and you're worth more alive to me than dead."

"Who wants me dead?" Grace asked, as Edmund grabbed her upper arm and pulled her out the door to go back up the hill to the house.

"Someone you trusted too much. And apparently, so did I."

SEVENTEEN

"There's no one around," Jack said, as he moved to the front of the sheriff's cruiser and waited for Hank. "This is the second time I've seen the place empty like this. I didn't like it the first time, and I don't like it now. But if my memory serves me right, I'll find the man I'm looking for somewhere around here."

"After the track accident, maybe Barone gave the crew time off until the operation is cleared of wrong-doing. I'm thinking you'll not find anyone. Why, exactly, do you think Grace is here?"

"I'm pretty sure the guy who drugged and stuffed me in the morgue this morning is someone I've seen here. I want to speak to the owner about him." Jack scanned the area. The big house on the hill drew his attention. "Ever been up there?" He pointed to it.

"Not as much as I used to, but sure. Ed Senior passed away a year ago and Edmund got permission from the attorney to stay there until the estate is worked out."

For now, Jack headed toward the stable, with the local lawman beside him.

Sheriff Maddox drew his gun.

Jack did the same.

The sheriff shook his head. "I would have never known. That's some cover you've got. But it's blown now, so why are you still dressed like an Amish person?"

"Maybe because the real cover was the FBI agent, and I just didn't realize it." The words came swift and clear, and in an instant, his heart knew it was true. He would always be Amish.

"Then lose the gun," Hank said, with a daring look in his eyes.

Jack froze at the idea. He stared down at the weapon in his hand that had been an extension of himself for so long. He might think he would always be Amish, but he would also be a fighter for those who needed help.

And Grace needed the FBI man right now.

Hank extended his hand. "For once, let me be the law around here."

Jack heard what the sheriff wasn't saying, when the man had every right to complain. Jack had jurisdiction over the stolen and transported horses, but the local law enforcement also had responsibilities to keep the peace. In Jack's quest for justice, he had overstepped his boundaries. "I apologize. Perhaps the people I care about most in this life wouldn't be hurt if I had brought you in. But until they are all safe and sound, I'll keep my sidearm at the ready."

Sheriff Maddox gave him a warning look. "Fine, but you'll follow my orders."

"Lead the way, Sheriff."

Jack accepted that this would be the last time he'd depend on his weapon. From here on out, he would return to the simple life of no violence. There would be no going back once he made this decision. The Amish way of life would come first forever. His only reliance would be on God and his community.

Hank eyed Jack as they approached the stable. He said warily, "This is not just another case for you, is it?"

Jack tore his gaze from his gun to look the sheriff in the eye. "This stopped being a case for me the day you found Benjamin in town. Somehow it became personal."

"That can be dangerous in this line of work, but I understand. You can't help how your heart will react."

Jack thought of the bishop's words. "*Ya*, I once followed my head, but this time I'm going to follow my heart."

When they reached the stable and stood at the door, Hank put a hand on Jack's arm. "I'll go in first to check things out. Follow close behind."

Jack adhered to the order and let him take the lead. Up until this point, Jack had handled things on his own, but now he would work with the sheriff.

Hank pressed the handle to open the stable door, but before he could pull them wide, the two wooden panels came bursting out at them. The high-pitched whinny of a horse on her hind legs pushed them back and had them lifting their arms in protection. The animal landed on her front hooves and bolted out to freedom. She galloped past them at full force and across the parking lot, not stopping until she came to a fence. Her sleek muscles rippled and twitched, and her tail swung wildly.

After taking a moment to catch their breaths, Hank looked at Jack and ushered him in silently. A horse loose in the stable set the stage for the unexpected inside. They could be walking into the aftermath of a horrid scene.

Please, Gött, let me find Grace alive, Jack prayed silently. The idea of losing her now, after finding his way back to his place in the Amish community, caused his stomach to clench. Physical pain shuddered through him, and he gripped at his left suspender over the location of his thudding heart.

The two men stepped inside and stood still, listening for any sounds of another person around. Other than a few horses rustling or huffing, no other noise was audible. Hank led the way down one aisle, each of them peering over the top of stalls, then down another. They returned to the entrance and checked the office.

"No one's here," Jack said, stepping from the small room, which held a few filing cabinets and a desk with a bunch of horse claims covering it. "I'd like to check the house."

Hank nodded. "We'll drive up."

The two of them went back to the cruiser and headed up the driveway to the sprawling house on the hill. As they turned the final bend and approached the side garages, Jack noticed one of them was open. The black sports car he had seen before was parked in the bay. "It looks like the owner is home."

They parked and exited the cruiser and went in through the garage. As Jack passed the sports car, he glanced inside and halted.

"Hold up," he said, and opened the driver's door. Pulling his sleeve over his hand, he reached across to the passenger seat and pulled out a long-haired black wig made from the tail of a horse. It was still fashioned into a ponytail from early that morning, when Jack had seen it last. Once again, his gut twisted. "Grace is here. Edmund Barone is our kidnapper, if not shooter and horse thief. I knew I'd seen his face around here."

"How can you be sure?"

"The man who used a tranquilizer on me was wearing this wig." He lifted it for the sheriff to see.

"Leave it there. We'll come back for it."

"Shouldn't you call for backup?"

"My backup is watching over your boss," Hank pointed out. "We're a small office. I'm going in. Stay close to me."

Jack dropped the wig back inside the car and shut the door with a soft click. He followed Sheriff Maddox up to the inside door. It opened without any problems into a large mudroom.

"County Sheriff's Office," Hank yelled. "We're coming in!"

Once inside, they made their way into a large kitchen and dining room. With each step across gleaming hardwood floors, Jack sensed they were being watched. He glanced toward the corners for surveillance, but if it was there, he couldn't see any without closer inspection.

Jack ran his finger across the dining room table. Dusty.

The place was beautiful, but he had to figure there was a whole crew for such a large spread. The fact that no one was around, and dust was allowed to settle on the sparse furnishings, told Jack the help had been let go.

He passed by sets of silverware rolled up in red cloth napkins that were placed haphazardly on a sideboard. It was as though someone had been putting them together one day and just stopped what they were doing and walked out. Judging by the dust on them, it was a while ago.

He moved across the room to another door. Staying off to one side, he carefully peered into the next room without making himself a target.

An enormous front hall with a chandelier stood empty of any furnishings. Two winding staircases on either side of the huge room extended up to a second floor with a circular railing between them. Jack retreated into the dining room, thinking there were too many places for someone to hide up there. Whether Hank wanted to admit it or not, they needed backup.

Jack glanced back, shaking his head about stepping out into the front hall, but Hank seemed to be busy rearranging the rolled silverware. Clearly, now was not the time. Was the man that fastidious? He waved the sheriff over, but as Hank approached, Jack noticed the napkins had been piled in a pyramid formation. He narrowed his eyes, trying to remember where he had seen such a thing before.

"I'll go first," Hank whispered loudly. "Stick close behind me."

Jack nodded, but his focus returned to the napkins. They were red, not yellow like the…corn.

He looked to the back of Hank's head as the man turned the corner into the large open room. The sheriff expected him to follow, but Jack stayed still as his brain flipped over the information he'd just remembered.

Hank had been the one arranging the corn into a pyramid that day at the Miller place. Which meant he hadn't picked Benjamin up in town as he had said.

Hank had been in the house with Benjamin.

And now he was leading Jack into the line of fire.

Just as Hank turned the corner and stepped out of sight, a deep-voiced shout came from outside the front of the house. "Are you in there, Grace?"

Jack's adrenaline spiked. "Benjamin?" he whispered, a feeling of dread filling him.

"No, *Daed*! It's a trap! Run!" Grace's voice echoed through the cavernous house, and the last word became muffled. She screamed through whatever was covering her mouth, then whimpered.

Jack didn't believe things could get any worse. Did he go to Benjamin? Did he run into the hall for Grace?

He had no choice but to go out there and help her. She and her *daed* would not survive if he didn't.

"What is it you want, Edmund?" Jack called, leaning against the wall behind him.

"Jack!" Grace cried but was quickly muffled once more. The desperation in her voice cut him to the quick.

He spoke out again, this time tilting his head out to glance around the front hall. "Do you want time to escape and go free from prosecution? You can have it. Just release the girl to her father. Let them walk out of here. You don't want them. They were just a means to an end to help you steal some horses. You can't use them anymore. So let them go."

Please.

"It's not that simple," a voice called from somewhere above him. "You see, my father left this place to my sister, Amelia Miller, which means Grace is in line to inherit it. All of it. I can't let that happen."

Jack sighed and leaned back again.

Things had just gotten worse.

EIGHTEEN

Grace struggled as Edmund held her in the upstairs hall with his hand over her mouth. From there, she could see her father through the large window. He stood on the patio with his shotgun in his hands. She could barely believe her eyes. After all his talk of turning the other cheek, he had come out to rescue her with a weapon. With her hands tied behind her with the riding crop Edmund had taken from the barn, she couldn't reach out to defend herself. But with her *daed* and Jack here, maybe there was still hope.

Or she could lose the two men she loved most in this world.

Edmund held her tightly, almost crushing the air from her lungs. The injury to her neck caused her vision to blur for a moment, but then the pain subsided. After several slow breaths her eyes cleared.

Grace struggled to free herself from Edmund's hold. She noticed that something on the lower floor held his attention. A glance through the spokes of the railing showed Sheriff Maddox entering the hall, gripping his gun.

A burst of hope filled Grace. Jack had brought the sheriff. She wanted to yell for Hank to see Edmund hiding above him at the top of the stairs. Then she noticed Jack was following the sheriff, close behind. He, too, had his gun drawn.

But he was pointing it at Hank.

No! her mind screamed. They must not see Edmund behind the columns, or know he was up here. Muffled as she was, she deliberately stumbled, making as much noise as she could. It was enough to make the men turn their weapons her way.

The next moment she felt like a horse had kicked her in her stomach. A shot rang out through the house, and Grace was thrown back against the wall. Seconds ticked by before her lungs refilled, and she realized she was free from Edmund's grasp. The riding crop he'd bound her with had fallen to the floor.

"Run," a gurgling voice whispered in her ear. Edmund.

Grace faced him and saw that he'd been shot. A tussle was happening downstairs, but all Grace could focus on was Edmund's moving lips.

"Hank wants you dead. He was engaged to your mother, but she left him for your father... Been waiting...a long time for...payback."

With that he took a final breath and let it slip out as he fell to the floor.

Grace shrank away from Edmund's dead body and processed all he'd told her.

Hank was the one who tried to kill her. And would again. That was why he had said she was never supposed to be born in the first place. Grace's fingers wrapped around the handle of the riding crop. But her father's words repeated in her mind.

No fight.

Before she could decide what to do, she heard Jack shout from below. "*Outen* the light," he cried. She looked down and saw him take another swing at the sheriff.

His order stumped her. The only lights were the four bulbs in the chandelier hanging over the enormous entrance hall.

The front door burst open wide and Benjamin stood there with the darkening sky behind him.

Turning toward the silhouette, Hank lifted his gun and pointed it at her *daed.* She shivered at the sight of the loaded weapon aimed at him. Her voice caught in her throat, and she couldn't utter a warning. Breath stalled in her chest as she braced for a gunshot.

Instead, she heard Sheriff Maddox's evil snort.

"On second thought, I'll let you watch your daughter die first. I wish you could have seen Amelia take her last breath. But this will work, too."

In the next second, Hank turned, aimed the gun at her and pulled the trigger.

Grace screamed, but quickly realized he'd missed. He shot again, and she pressed back against the wall to avoid taking the bullet.

She heard Jack shout something she couldn't make out for the fear pounding in her head, then she leaned forward to see the two lawmen on the floor, still fighting.

"*Outen* the light!" Jack shouted again. But this time, she understood.

"Ya, ich verschteh." She understood perfectly. She picked up the riding crop and flicked it at the chandelier straight ahead of her. It smashed a lightbulb and wrapped a few times around one of the ornate branches. She yanked it back, but it snagged and turned the whole chandelier to the left. Grace pulled again, and finally it released.

She swung the riding crop again, aiming for another light and smashing it the same way. One by one, all four bulbs were extinguished, finally plunging the space into darkness.

Grace turned and crawled to the opposite staircase. Jack fighting Hank for the gun filled the hall with the sounds of grunts and smacks. Grace cringed at each one as, pressing herself to the railing, she slipped down the stairs toward the front door and her *daed.*

At the base of the stairs, she could make out the men's silhouettes in the moonlight cascading through the windows. She reached Benjamin and moved him toward the wall behind her so they could slide by Jack and Hank.

The door beckoned, only a few feet away. She grasped the cotton fabric of her father's shirt and pulled him with her, but just as she reached the door and curled her hand around the knob a bang close to her ear jolted her back and away. Grace fell to the floor, her head ringing from the sound. Slowly, she turned to find her *daed*, but he wasn't beside her anymore. She hoped he hadn't been hit.

Just as she spotted him a loud creak echoed through the room, then everyone stilled, even the two men fighting. Grace held her breath for a moment of uncertainty.

Her body ached.

Her ears questioned the eerie and strange creaking sound.

And time stood still…

Grace felt the rush of wind before she heard the crash. It was warning enough for her to lift her arm and instinctively shield her face. The sound of millions of glass fragments splintering and flying through the air filled the space, and Grace knew instantly the chandelier had come falling down on them.

She knew without moving that many of those glass pieces were embedded in her clothing and even in her skin. She hoped her father, closer to a wall, had escaped the worst of it. It was the deathly silence from the middle of the room that scared her the most.

Jack.

Grace heard a cry and quickly realized it had slipped from her own lips. Covering her trembling mouth, she took a step toward the center of the room.

Glass crackled beneath her boots, the only sound. "Jack? Are you there?" Hearing no response, she stepped back to her father. *"Komm,"* she instructed him, and together they exited the house. She placed him behind one of the large planters. "Sit and wait for me. I have to go help Jack."

"Amos?" Benjamin said.

"No, *Daed*. He's not your *brudder*. He's Jack, *die mann ich lieb*." The man I love. Saying the words that she had been denying since the moment she'd wanted Jack to kiss her in the barn brought a sense of peace that could only be from God.

But admitting her love for this man would go nowhere—even if he was alive.

Benjamin took her hand in his. *"Lieb, ya?"*

"Ya," she said. She loved him. No matter where her life led, or who she would have to marry, in her heart she would always love Jack Kaufman.

"Neigeh," her father told her. Go in. She nodded, but as she turned, he pulled her hand back and said, *"Zu der maedel geh."* He was giving them permission to court.

Grace tried to smile through a frown. Her *daed* didn't understand that he could never court her. He wasn't Amish anymore, and she always would be. She left her father to step back inside.

Still no sound could be heard but leaving the door open to let in a little more moonlight, she could make out the fallen chandelier. She circled around it until her foot hit something. Or someone.

It could be Jack, or it could be Hank.

Suddenly, a light flashed on ahead of her, and she could see Jack holding his phone.

"Jack!" She headed that way, bending over to try to lift the chandelier when she saw his leg caught beneath it.

"Be careful. It's heavy. Don't cut yourself." He groaned as she shifted the broken metal fixture. "Where's Hank?"

She looked back to the body she'd literally stumbled upon. "He's over there, and oh! He's moving a little. He's alive."

"Good. He'll need to stand trial for murder, as well as framing me for the crime."

"What do you mean?"

"He used my gun to kill Barone and would have used it on you and Benjamin. Then he could have shot me with his own gun and said he caught me in the act."

Grace lifted the chandelier a little, but it was enough for Jack to pull himself free. Each movement he made elicited more groans as he slowly got to his feet.

"There's glass everywhere," she said.

"I see that *and* feel it." He lifted his phone and used the light to find and secure the two guns. Then he punched in a number. When someone answered, he reported the situation and requested law enforcement.

Then he held the light over Hank, one of their own. Such a shame.

The sheriff was hurt badly and wasn't going anywhere. Jack felt for his pulse, then stood back up. "The police can deal with him. Let's go get your *daed*."

"Shouldn't you stay to arrest him?"

"We'll be outside to answer questions, but this is not my case anymore."

"Why not?" she asked, coming up alongside him to help him walk. They carefully wrapped an arm around each other as they crossed the threshold.

"I quit the FBI."

Grace halted and stared up at him. "You can do that?"

Jack chuckled. "I'm going to have to if I'm Amish. I can't do both."

Grace stood *ferhoodled*. Did he really mean that? "Are you going back to Colorado?"

"No, *lieb*. I'm staying here. With you." He swallowed and tensed beside her. "I mean, if you'll have me. I would like to court you."

"Court?" she asked warily.

He smiled nervously in the moonlight. "And by court, I mean marry. I'm sorry, I'm not very good at this. It will take some time for me to learn how to be a *gut mann* for you. I've been running for a long time. Following my head instead of my heart."

Grace smiled and reached for a small piece of glass in his face. "That's just fine, because it will take me some time to learn how to be a *gut frau* for you."

He grabbed her hand in his. He was cut up badly, but she held him gently "I don't want you to change for me. I want you to do what your heart longs for."

"My heart longs for you, Jack."

"And the *gauls*. Don't forget the horses." He smiled. "You're a natural. Watching you in the stands, I could tell. Don't give it up for me."

Grace's heart filled to bursting. Could she really have both loves in her life? "Your gift is *wunderbar. Denki*." Without thinking, she rose up on her toes and found Jack's lips in gratitude.

It quickly turned to a kiss of love that curled her toes. More perfect than she could have ever imagined.

In shock at her boldness, she stepped back. "I'm sor—"

Jack reached for her and leaned down to capture her mouth again before she could apologize. She smiled against his lips, accepting this moment as confirmation that waiting to marry for love would make all the difference.

The sound of a throat being cleared interrupted them. "Excuse me, but you're *bussing* my daughter."

They pulled apart and turned to face her *daed.* And found another figure standing beside him.

Police sirens floated through the night as Grace and Jack studied the frightened-looking young man.

"Liam," Grace said. "Did you know about all this?"

He shook his head. "I'm sorry. I believed him when he said he wanted to bring you home. I didn't know he planned to kill you so he would inherit the place. He said he was making things right, but I see now he meant right for him." Liam looked to Jack, his worried eyes glinting in the moonlight. "Sir, I would like to turn myself in for swapping the horses in the stables and stealing them from the Millers' farm afterward. And for shooting you."

Jack nodded. "That's right mature of you, Liam, but I will let the local law enforcement handle things from here on in."

"Jack?" Grace said, placing her hand on his forearm. "Would it be all right if we speak for Liam? So the authorities know Edmund and Hank both used a lot of people to accomplish their goals."

Jack leaned over and kissed her temple gently. "I think that's possible," he whispered, loudly enough for Liam to hear.

The young man glanced from one to the other, his turn to be *ferhoodled.* "I don't understand. Why would you do that? I could have killed you."

Jack winced as he wrapped a gingerly arm around Grace. "You see, Liam, it's called grace. Accept it and be thankful. It's a gift that doesn't come around very often, but it's powerful enough to change your life for the better and give you your heart's desire." He gazed down at Grace with shining his eyes. "I should know. Grace brought me home."

Liam huffed. "Yeah, well, speaking of homes, what are you going to do with this place? Will you live here?"

"No," Grace said. "Why would we live here? It's much too fancy for the plain life."

"But you own it. Mr. Barone left it to you when he died. Well, he left it to your mother." Liam frowned, not commenting on how her *mamm*'s life had been cut short over money and property.

Grace thought about it for a moment. She had no idea what she would do with such an inheritance.

Three cruisers raced into the lot and up the driveway to take over the case. The night would belong to them from then on, and any decisions about the future of Autumn Woods could come later.

For now, Grace reached for her *daed* with one arm and held on to her future *mann* with the other. The road ahead wouldn't be easy, but she would walk it with faith, hope and love. And on some days, she might even trot along with a *gut gaul*.

EPILOGUE

Summer at Autumn Woods brought out the beautiful horses to graze, but the ranch also welcomed families and loved ones of people with dementia and Alzheimer's.

Grace had donated the grounds and buildings to be used as a home and day care facility for people living with these illnesses. Even the horses were part of the deal, with the agreement that the Amish would also be welcome.

Benjamin Miller walked over to a group around Game Changer, while Grace and Jack hung back near the fence. They watched as residents groomed the horses and spend time with the sweet-natured creatures.

"Game Changer's taken a liking to *daed*," Grace said. "She will make a *gut* friend to him here on his visiting days and when...this becomes his home someday."

Jack placed a hand on her shoulder. "That won't be for a long time, *lieb*."

"He doesn't know me today," she said quietly, and squeezed back the tears forming in her eyes. "He hasn't known me for a few days now. And his gait is different. He'll need a wheelchair soon."

"He'll have whatever he needs. This place will help, and so will our community. You just worry about loving him. And as for not knowing you," Jack added, as he took her hand and squeezed it, "I have to think that somewhere inside his heart he does." He turned her to face him, but with her round belly filled with child, they could get only so close. "You're giving him the best life here. Now, during the days, and later, if and when he needs to come here to stay permanently. We'll never be far away and will be here regularly to see him."

"I want to be the one to take care of him," Grace said. "It's the Amish way to care for family and community throughout life."

"The bishop has given his blessing if we find we can't. The facility can provide things you can't for his health. They can help us give him a better life for his remaining days. Maybe even time to meet his *kinner*."

Grace took comfort in this fact and wished her *mamm* had had the same opportunity, but all Grace could do was focus on the track ahead. Her race wasn't complete yet, but with God's guidance and provision, and with eyes fixed on Him, she would finish it well.

She gazed up at her *mann.* She couldn't think of a better partner to run the race with. And soon they would leave for Colorado, where she would be by his side while he made amends with his old community. After the *boppli* arrived and could make the trip, they would spend a few weeks in the mountains. Grace looked forward to seeing where her *mann* grew up. And no matter the outcome with his family and friends, she vowed to always stand by him as he had always done for her, even when he thought she might be a criminal.

Grace giggled.

"What's so funny?" Jack touched her nose and asked.

"I was just thinking how close I came to a life behind bars."

"Hey, don't laugh. The idea gives me nightmares just thinking about it. Although I'm certain sure Nic would have laughed at me when I brought you in in cuffs. She wouldn't have let you go down for the crime."

"Is she planning to come meet the *boppli* when he or she is born?"

"Just try and stop her. But be warned, her idea of gifts might be boxing gloves."

"Ach, no. No *fechde*."

"Right, no fighting. I'll remember that eventually. I think I'm doing well. Even when I went after Hank, it wasn't to hurt him. It was only to get the gun out of his hands."

Grace frowned at how close she had come to losing the man she loved. "I pray nothing like that ever happens again."

"And now that Hank is put away for life, and Sheriff Shaw is running the county, I feel certain sure it won't."

Suddenly, Grace remembered something she wanted to share with her life partner. In her excitement, she reached up and pulled on her *kapp*'s strings. "I read in *The Budget* that Liam will be released early on good behavior and, listen to this, Leroy is to be married."

"Gut!" Jack pressed his lips together to suppress a smile. He pulled one of her straps from her hand and

wound it through his fingers. His eyes shined with joy and mischief. "Now we don't have to worry about him coming after us for revenge someday."

Grace jabbed her *mann* with her elbow in a joking way. "He hardly would have ever done such a thing."

Jack let his smile spread and leaned close to capture her gaze. "I think you don't have any idea how *wunderbar* you are. Let me tell you so you know."

"Ya?" Grace felt her cheeks flush. Funny how this man could still make her feel this way.

"*Ya*, Mrs. Kaufman, you are a blessing from *Gött.* Your free gift of grace changed me and how I saw myself. You bring hope and healing to me and to those you meet. And I will forever be grateful for the day I held you at gunpoint."

Grace burst out in a jubilant laugh. She reached for his hand still holding her strap, never wanting to let go of her *mann.* "I must be *ferhoodled*, because, Mr. Kaufman, so will I. So will I."

And with that, Jack pressed a sweet kiss to her lips, a kiss filled with promises and love for their race to the finish line.

* * * * *

Dear Reader,

I enjoy traveling to new places and meeting new people, especially when those people live such different lifestyles than I am used to. Writing about the Amish people meant taking a trip to an Amish community. I spent a whole day meeting some of the kindest and gentlest people I've ever met. One neat thing I enjoyed learning about them is they also love to read. I felt closer to them instantly.

I am glad to introduce you to Jack and Grace in the pages of *Amish Country Undercover.* I hope their story of redemption and second chances warms your heart, but I also hope the excitement and suspense keep those pages turning lightning quick. Grace's love for horses endeared her to me, and I hope you love that trait about her, too.

I love to hear from readers, and you can reach me through email at KatyLee@KatyLeeBooks.com or through Facebook, Instagram and Twitter. My website is KatyLeeBooks.com.

Happy reading!
Katy Lee

COMING NEXT MONTH FROM
Love Inspired Suspense

Available March 3, 2020

FUGITIVE TRAIL
K-9 Mountain Guardians • by Elizabeth Goddard

When an escaped convict vows revenge on Deputy Sierra Young, former coworker turned PI Bryce Elliott is determined to protect her. But can Bryce, Sierra and her search-and-rescue K-9, Samson, track the fugitive before he succeeds in taking their lives?

FALSELY ACCUSED
FBI: Special Crimes Unit • by Shirlee McCoy

Framed for her foster brother's murder, FBI special agent Wren Santino must clear her name—but someone's dead set on stopping her from finding the truth. Now with help from her childhood friend Titus Anderson, unraveling a conspiracy may be the only way to survive.

AMISH COUNTRY MURDER
by Mary Alford

As the sole woman to escape the Dead of Night Killer, Catherine Fisher's the key to catching him—if he doesn't kill her first. But with her memory missing and all clues indicating the serial killer targeted her for very personal reasons, it'll take everything FBI agent Sutter Brenneman has to keep her safe.

MOUNTAIN CAPTIVE
by Sharon Dunn

Private investigator Jude Trainor won't give up on finding a kidnapped little girl—even when the suspect runs him off a mountain road and sends bullets his way. But when Lacey Conrad rescues Jude on her snowmobile, can they outlast a snowstorm *and* a person who wants them dead?

STOLEN SECRETS
by Sherri Shackelford

After she discovers someone's been impersonating her to steal classified technology secrets, Lucy Sutton has to figure out who's behind it. National Security Agency employee Jordan Harris is the only person she trusts. But capturing the culprit is an even deadlier task than they expected.

KILLER HARVEST
by Tanya Stowe

With her boss murdered, Sassa Nilsson's the last person who can save the world's crops from a lethal plant pathogen. But with criminals willing to kill Sassa to get the formula for the virus, can border patrol agent Jared De Luca shield her?

LOOK FOR THESE AND OTHER LOVE INSPIRED BOOKS WHEREVER BOOKS ARE SOLD, INCLUDING MOST BOOKSTORES, SUPERMARKETS, DISCOUNT STORES AND DRUGSTORES.

LISCNM0220

SPECIAL EXCERPT FROM

Framed for her foster brother's murder, FBI special agent Wren Santino must clear her name—but someone's dead set on stopping her from finding the truth. Now with help from her childhood friend Titus Anderson, unraveling a conspiracy may be the only way to survive.

Read on for a sneak preview of Falsely Accused *by Shirlee McCoy, available March 2020 from Love Inspired Suspense!*

Titus turned onto the paved road that led to town. Wren had said Ryan was there. Ambushed by the men who'd been trying to kill her.

He glanced in his rearview mirror and saw a car coming up fast behind him. No headlights. Just white paint gleaming in the moonlight.

"What's wrong?" Wren asked, shifting to look out the back window. "That's them," she murmured, her voice cold with anger or fear.

"Good. Let's see if we can lead them to the police."

"They'll run us off the road before then."

Probably, but the closer they were to help when it happened, the better off they'd be. He sped around a curve in the road, the white car closing the gap between them. It tapped his bumper, knocking the Jeep sideways.

He straightened, steering the Jeep back onto the road, and tried to accelerate into the next curve as he was rear-ended again.

This time, the force of the impact sent him spinning out of control. The Jeep glanced off a guardrail, bounced back onto the road and then off it, tumbling down into a creek and landing nose down in the soft creek bed.

He didn't have time to think about damage, to ask if Wren was okay or to make another call to 911. He knew the men in the car were going to come for them.

Come for *Wren*.

And he was going to make certain they didn't get her.

Don't miss
Falsely Accused *by Shirlee McCoy,*
available March 2020 wherever
Love Inspired Suspense books and ebooks are sold.

LoveInspired.com

LISEXP0220

Can the new teacher in this Amish community help the family next door without losing her heart?

Read on for a sneak preview of The Amish Teacher's Dilemma *by Patricia Davids, available in March 2020 from Love Inspired.*

Clang, clang, clang.

The hammering outside her new schoolhouse grew louder. Eva Coblentz moved to the window to locate the source of the clatter. Across the road she saw a man pounding on an ancient-looking piece of machinery with steel wheels and a scoop-like nose on the front end.

When he had the sheet of metal shaped to fit the front of the machine, he stood back to assess his work. He knelt and hammered on the shovel-like nose three more times. Satisfied, he gathered up his tools and started in her direction.

She stepped back from the window. Was he coming to the school? Why? Had he noticed her gawking? Perhaps he only wanted to welcome the new teacher, although his lack of a beard said he wasn't married.

She glanced around the room. Should she meet him by the door? That seemed too eager. Her eyes settled on the large desk at the front of the classroom. She should look as if she was ready for the school year to start. A professional attitude would put off any suggestion that she was interested in meeting single men.

LIEXP0220

Eva hurried to the desk, pulled out the chair and sat down as the outside door opened. The chair tipped over backward, sending her flailing. Her head hit the wall with a painful thud as she slid to the floor. Stunned, she slowly opened her eyes to see the man leaning over the desk.

He had the most beautiful gray eyes she'd ever beheld. They were rimmed with thick, dark lashes in stark contrast to the mop of curly, dark red hair springing out from beneath his straw hat. Tiny sparks of light whirled around him.

"I'm Willis Gingrich. Local blacksmith." He squatted beside her. "Can you tell me your name?"

The warmth and strength of his hand on her skin sent a sizzle of awareness along her nerve endings. "I'm Eva Coblentz. I am the new teacher and I'm fine now."

LIEXP0220